Mr. and Mrs. Justice:
A Supreme Court Love Story

Gary R. Ryman

Copyright © 2023 Gary Ryman. All rights reserved. Including the right to reproduce this book or portions thereof, in any form. No part of this text may be reproduced in any form without the express written permission of the author.

Version 2017.03.01

ISBN: 9798859817382

Lakeland Press

Dedication:
To Michelle, Michael, and Megan

1

I disliked that first Monday in October the way a ten-year-old hated the start of the school year. Walking into my chambers for the first formal day of my fifteenth term, I shrugged off my rain-sodden overcoat. Inside my well-worn leather briefcase, apart from a pad of sticky notes and my cell phone, was a peanut butter and jelly sandwich and two cookies. Probably not much different than what the ten-year-old had in his backpack. Rather ironic, and not what the public would expect from a sitting Justice of the Supreme Court of the United States.

"Good morning, Justice Cashman," my secretary said from behind her desk, which she kept strategically positioned to guard the entrance to my office, half Buckingham Palace guard, half pit bull. She had watched over this doorway not only for my entire time on the court, but for that of my predecessor as well. Her formal title was Senior Administrative Assistant in the modern politically correct terminology, but since justices have had secretaries since the 1800s, I preferred the legacy title and luckily so did she.

"And good morning to you, Edith," I said.

"Would you care for some tea and toast, sir?" I had breakfasted on tea and toast perhaps twice in my years on the court, yet received the same menu offering each morning. By now, one would have thought she knew I was an English muffin and decaf man.

"No, thank you, Edith; just the usual this morning."

"Very good, I'll send it in immediately," she said.

I had my one cup of regular coffee at home to jump start myself, consumed after my shower and shave while I flipped through the channels looking for the least irritating morning news and the local traffic report to gauge whether my five-mile commute would take ten minutes or an hour. More caffeine than that, I'd found, would irritate my stomach on the ride in. As the commute and my job could do that quite well on their own, there was little sense giving the erosion of my stomach lining unneeded assistance.

Although today was the formal start of the term when we'd hear our first case, I'd been in chambers regularly for the past month, but the clerks had been there since July after relieving last term's team. Our multi-day "long conference" at which we voted on which cases to accept to fill out a few spots on the calendar for the coming term had been completed in September with the usual drudgery. It takes four of us desiring to hear a case to grant certiorari or "cert," as we call it. Each justice has their own criteria, hot buttons, and sometimes even strategies for deciding what cases they want to grant.

Much of the preliminary work was done by the clerks who sorted through the thousands of petitions, winnowing out the wheat from the chaff. It really came down to a couple hundred which presented compelling issues from which we would select maybe a half dozen. Around thirty cases had already been granted or carried over from the previous term. We would add another ten or so that we would hear this year as this one progressed. We would ultimately hear and decide between fifty and seventy cases in an average term. Although the justices take exception to accusations that they don't work very hard and take all summer off, I freely admit the workload is far from burdensome.

My jaded mood hadn't just started this morning. The end of the previous term was disappointing, being on the losing side of most of the term's biggest decisions. My malaise carried over to the long conference, where I could not summon much enthusiasm about many of the cases proposed for the docket. I withheld my vote from all but three, surprising the brethren as I still called them, even with the presence of several women on the court.

I settled into the tufted burgundy leather chair behind my antique wooden desk. The desk had been used by Justice Souter, one of my judicial heroes, mainly known to the public for disappointing the president who appointed him, an admirable trait in my opinion. His initials were scratched into one of the drawers along with some others, presumably his predecessors who had used the desk, but I'd never researched who else had sat behind it. I might scratch my own in there someday if I got bored and could smuggle anything bigger than fingernail trimmers past the metal detectors.

Another reason I was so fond of Justice Souter is he didn't take this lifetime appointment stuff seriously. He served for a good many years, then while still in excellent health, and young in judge years (a Supreme Court Justice is still considered young into their mid-seventies), retired back to the rural New Hampshire he loved. Smart man.

Edith brought in my English muffin, burnt of course from the ancient toaster she kept in the outer office, matching my mood, and the coffee. The coffee wasn't cold as expected, but it was as weak as the tea she offered me each morning. I added some extra jelly to the muffin and consumed it and the coffee without complaint while glancing through the *Washington Post*. There was one long article which caught my eye, providing a preview of our coming term and prognostication of what the reporter believed would be the most noteworthy cases.

The article was, in my mind, no more than half right. It talked about a few cases we had granted last June for this term and some that had been under consideration at the long conference. A few of the term's sexy cases would probably come out 5-4, I thought, but not necessarily the ones the article talked about. Some listed as a sure thing for inclusion on the docket I knew we hadn't taken; decisions which would be announced about two hours from now. I turned to the sports section where the news might be more accurate, football scores being difficult to get wrong.

Another beginning of term tradition was our group photo. We gathered in front of a curtain; the chief and four justices sitting, and the others standing behind, like most things we do, in order of seniority. These were done each year whether the court membership changed or not. The photo reminded me of the ones from my elementary school days I found saved in a drawer while cleaning out my mother's house after her passing. There I was with my first-grade class, second grade, third grade, and so on. A few changes here and there, but mostly the same kids, just like the nine of us now. And getting the photo taken here was the same amount of fun; me with the same forced smile on my face, fifty plus years later.

"Excuse me, Justice Cashman, here are the briefs for the next sitting," Leslie Jacobs, one of my clerks for this term walked across the room and set the eighteen-inch stack of files with their multi-colored covers down on the work table next to my desk. These would be some of the November cases.

"Thank you, Leslie. Have you and the boys had coffee yet?"

"No sir."

"Well gather them up and come in and ask Edith to send for a pot; the real stuff this time, not this tea water I've been drinking." I knew it would still be decaf, but Edith would get it from the court cafeteria, so it would be better than what came out of the tiny Mr. Coffee she kept behind her desk.

While Leslie gathered the troops and the coffee, I opened the bench memo for the first case we'd be hearing this morning. I shook my head. It was not my idea of how to open the term.

The maker of a children's game called "Kerplunk" argued trademark and copyright infringement over the ridiculous name. *Kerplunk v. Forest, et.al.* was the official name of the case. The circuit court was closely divided on the subject and four of my colleagues thought the question important enough for us to decide. The toy company claimed hundreds of millions of dollars for use of the name from thousands of different users, most of whom had used the word simply as a sound effect. My vote would be to reverse the circuit court which had upheld the ridiculous claims in a clumsily reasoned opinion.

It may come as a surprise, but oral argument was, at least for me, a formality to be endured. The arguments of the lawyers, when we actually let them talk, didn't change my initial inclination on how I would vote on a case more than once every few years. Most of my colleagues however, enjoyed the give-and-take with the attorneys, particularly the questions and hypotheticals they posed to both sides. Many of my fellow justices spent some portion of their career as law professors, so it brought them back to the classroom, interrogating trembling law students. They would also admit that oral argument didn't change their mind either in most cases, but that didn't stop the interminable questioning and interruptions.

The bench memo couldn't hold my attention while I waited for the clerks and coffee. I'd reread it thoroughly for at least the third time, along with the briefs in the case, over the weekend. It wasn't like I had anything else to do. That was another reason why I wasn't looking forward to the new term.

The reason I had nothing to do but read briefs and memos on a sunny crisp fall weekend was that my wife had left me at the end of the previous term. She was my third wife, and our divorce was uncomplicated as I had been through this before, and prepared accordingly before our wedding two years ago, with an iron clad pre-nuptial agreement on which her signature rested. There were no children from the union. I'd covered that life experience with my first wife, with whom I remained on good terms. Wife number one was a wonderful woman and great mother; we just couldn't live together, mostly because I had put my job first.

Wife number three turned out to be not exactly a prize. She could be described, and I know was, at least in the *Washington Post* gossip column, as a trophy wife. Younger than me by twenty years, blonde and buxom, quite good looking she was, *trophy* she was not. Even so, I missed her, or to be honest, missed having someone to come home to, even with the continual disagreements. Maybe I just sucked at marriage?

She was water under the bridge and it was time to get my head back in the game, and a few other metaphors, with the start of the new term.

Edith came in pushing a cart, with a pot of coffee, five cups, creamer, sugar, and stirring implements; the clerks entering behind her like chicks following the mother hen.

"Stay, Edith, and have a cup with us," I said, knowing I would get the same standard answer as I gave with her tea question, having asked it almost as many times.

"No, thank you, Mr. Justice. You have important work to do with these young people."

The cups were distributed and coffee served with requisite amounts of sugar and creamer to personal taste.

"Thoughts on *Kerplunk*?" I opened the discussion. Each clerk had cases they were primarily responsible for, which included preparation of a bench memo for me, and a first draft of a full opinion, dissent, or concurrence, if I ended up writing on the case. Beyond that, they were to be familiar with all the cases so we could discuss them as a group. I wanted a diversity of opinion within a collegial environment. Easy to say. More difficult to do. This one was Leslie's.

"I think it's clear the 9th Circuit overreached and their opinion arguably twists precedent," she said.

"My reading is some of the other justices may not see it that way," John offered. Leslie bristled, but didn't say anything. Among the clerks this term, John led the way in developing relationships with his counterparts in the other chambers, establishing my pseudo intelligence apparatus for the term.

"I think you're both right," I said. "Not a great way to start the term, but we shall see. Did anyone see the Redskins or Commanders, or whatever their name is this week, game yesterday?" Might as well talk about an even less pleasant subject, the hated Cowboys having dismantled our team 35-3. I looked at my watch while half listening to the chatter among the clerks on the game. It approached robing time.

"Well, I must be off. Time to watch his Royal Highness don his ridiculous striped monstrosity. One wonders if this year he'll switch to ermine or add a crown and scepter," I said with my poor version of a British accent.

The group chuckled politely at my indiscreet and less than charitable view of the chief justice and his outlandish striped robe. He had taken the practice from Chief Justice Rehnquist but made the four gold stripes on each sleeve wider and brighter. If they grew any larger, our chief could moonlight summers as a flagger on highway construction projects.

In the robing room, which was like a high-end country club locker room with immaculate high gloss wooden lockers and plush carpet, each justice greeted the others with a handshake before donning their robe, a practice that went back over a century, although the unanimity of it was dependent upon the relationships between the brethren at various times of history. Luckily, we all got along. We then lined up in the appropriate order of seniority, which was how we sat on the bench, to enter the courtroom.

The absent-minded professor, Chief Justice David Palmetto, called the court to order, only ten minutes late, which was a record for him. The first part, the reading of the orders noting which cases we'd accepted, required me to display some modicum of interest and attention to the court's business. The same with the admission of lawyers to the Supreme Court bar. Both were formalities but, tradition dictated we try to avoid sleeping through them.

Finally, around 11:15 AM, he called the first case. Chuckles rippled through those in attendance at hearing the word "Kerplunk" uttered in the Supreme Court of the United States, particularly as the plaintiff in a dispute.

The attorney representing Kerplunk, not one of our regulars, managed to get out "Mr. Chief Justice and may it please the court," before he was hit with the first question from the bench.

This allowed me to begin my normal routine while on the bench; playing games on my phone. Most of the other justices assumed I was answering email. The media and public thought I was an inveterate note taker. Only my neighbor to the right, Justice Antonia Romaldini, or Romo to me, knew what I was really doing. Occasionally she would glance over and roll her eyes at my activities, interpreted by most in the audience who noticed as a comment on the argument of whatever lawyer was speaking at the time. Typically, I could conquer four or five games over the course of a term.

Early on I had adopted the practice of one of my predecessors, Justice Clarence Thomas, who, until Covid, asked a record low five or so questions over his first thirty years on the court. That number may not be precise as I didn't waste the time to look it up, but it's damn close. Chief Justice Roberts changed the process during the pandemic to facilitate "Zoom" court sessions, giving each justice a set time to ask questions in order of seniority, which almost forced Thomas to say something. After the brethren returned to the bench, Roberts continued a hybrid of the process, perhaps liking it better than the free-for-all that previously had been in place. Chief Justice Palmetto eliminated the Roberts revisions, and reverted to chaos, in my opinion.

I wasn't quite as silent as Thomas, but it was close. A few times a term, though, as I listened, I would hear a lawyer utter something so egregious, so ridiculous that I would be unable to help myself and would pop off with a question or short hypothetical; usually resulting in me having to start over whatever level I was on in the game underway at the time. My question would invariably result in a comment in whatever article the various supreme court press reporters were writing for their respective outlets. One blog literally kept a running tally of my comments and questions each term. The individual in charge had far too much time on their hands.

As the rapid-fire questioning of Kerplunk's counsel began, I fired up *Hitman Go* on my phone. Killing a few people this morning seemed like great fun.

Kerplunk passed painlessly and the unmemorable tax case we heard in the afternoon was a snoozer, but it allowed me to complete the first level on my game, an auspicious beginning. Back in chambers, around five in the afternoon or evening, depending upon how you view the day, I poured two fingers of whiskey into a heavy cut glass tumbler, added an ice cube, and in a blasphemous act, a small splash of 7-Up. I kicked my feet up on my desk. The clerks trooped in and I waved them to the bar where they each selected and poured a beverage of choice. They gathered round so we could discuss the day's oral arguments. Surprisingly, at least to me, the boys were teetotalers, but Leslie was happy to join me and share a cocktail. They had more opinions than I; only the highpoints having penetrated my attention to the Hitman game.

Halfway through my second drink, I noticed that Leslie was a quite attractive young lady. Maybe it was when she let her hair down, or after I consumed a couple ounces of alcohol. Obviously, anything beyond simply noticing was non-starter. Although my wives had been getting younger, there was a hard limit, and younger than my daughter was miles over that line. And that was before issues of workplace propriety, etc. were considered. I hoped that when my blood alcohol dropped to below DUI levels, my inappropriate evaluation of my female clerk's attributes would similarly fade. I did conclude, however, that some young lawyer, doctor, or government bureaucrat would be lucky to get a smart girl like her.

Resting on my desk to the right of the highball glass was a new book on the inner workings of the court. Books on the Supreme Court seem to be divided into three categories. First, there are those by journalists who develop access to documents, personal papers, and usually a few indiscreet ex-clerks or even an occasional justice themselves. With the sources on background and an incomplete documentary record, the result is always inaccurate. It is easy to settle past scores and leave a distorted view of events and the workings of the court. The second kind is issue-driven, with the author trying to show how erroneous an entire area of Supreme Court decisions is or just calling us out on a single major case. The third type is written by one of the justices themselves and is typically a history of one or more of their predecessors, or a work touting the correctness of their decisional process. Originalism, textualism, and the living constitution, have all been covered ad nauseum. There is seldom any introspection on their own service or time on the court, at least on any critical level.

The book you're reading, mine, falls into none of those categories. Sitting justices don't write about recent events. Hell, even the ones on their predecessors typically go back to when opinions were written with quill pens, and have all kinds of disclaimers. I didn't want to write one of those. I love all my fellow justices. (Okay, I had to have a couple drinks to write that sentence, but I left it in, so I must mean it.) Honestly, they are all good people. But as my contribution to the nation's civics lessons, I wanted to give an unvarnished look at how things work here, during what turned out to be an unusual term…and maybe make a couple bucks as well.

The book on my desk was one of the first type, and covered the period of my appointment to the court. I was the third choice of the president who appointed me—not an auspicious beginning. The first candidate withdrew when his fondness for marijuana was discovered. Not puffing a few joints as an undergrad or rolling a reefer during law school. No, this Circuit Court judge was growing the stuff in a spare bedroom of his house.

The Senate defeated the nomination of the second candidate when it was revealed she had a nanny problem. It wasn't that she was paying the illegal immigrant under the table—she was, but those transgressions are now considered minor recordkeeping errors rather than disqualifying events. No, it was when it was revealed she was sleeping with the nanny that the trouble began. Some senators viewed this as an inappropriate workplace practice, patently ignoring the number of secretaries and aides they regularly bedded. A few others were unadmitted racist homophobes, having a hard time picturing the lily-white Jewish lady judge in bed with the dark skinned Honduran illegal immigrant. You had to wonder how the dim bulbs missed this the year before when they'd unanimously confirmed her for a seat on the 7th Circuit. Luckily for me, when my name was put forward, I was still married to my first wife, with no gardening habit, illicit or otherwise.

I was an unusual selection in another way. I came from the state bench, not one of the federal circuits. I served on the Pennsylvania Supreme Court, one not known for producing many headlines beyond indictments of its members. During my tenure, I watched colleagues be convicted for use of staff for political purposes, and resignations for exchanging what we'll delicately call inappropriate material—okay, porn—on their state email accounts. Our holiday parties were fun, though.

Avoiding those improprieties made the senators from our fine commonwealth believe that made me a paradigm of virtuosity and suggested my name to a President desperate for a body to fill a black robe. I've heard since that following my multiple divorces and a few mentions in the gossip columns that the *Washington Post* characterizes as society pages, of an occasion or two of conspicuous consumption of adult beverages, that both Senators now regret their recommendation.

Of course, I would never think to mention the well-known relationship between the octogenarian senior senator from my state and his thirty something year old legislative assistant or the three driving under the influence arrests of the younger senator, which were swept under the rug by the District of Columbia police where he ardently supports the Metropolitan Police union and regularly speaks at their events. No, I would not mention such things.

As a state judge, I handled few of the issues commonly seen on the federal bench. That made my confirmation easier, as there was little for the Judiciary Committee members to nitpick in the way of opinions. Conversely it also gave some of the more rabid members ammunition, as they were able to play the inexperience card that I hadn't handled federal constitutional issues. Overall, though, I think the committee was just glad to have what looked to them like a vanilla nominee without skeletons, or marijuana plants, in their closet. The full Senate subsequently confirmed me, but it was far from unanimous.

My first few terms on the court were challenging dealing with true constitutional cases. That doesn't mean every case was like starting law school again, far from it. A good percentage of the cases we take each year are straight statutory interpretation, which all judges deal with on one level or another. You don't need to be Felix freaking Frankfurter to decide these. No, the challenge came from the half dozen or so cases we take every year which are controversial constitutional items. They change over time, but many involved race, sex, life, death; not unimportant items for the population at large. They are also the type of cases where the talking heads on television find it easy to take very black or white positions, further inflaming the rhetoric.

But I digress. A glass or two of whiskey or bourbon, I've found, is an amazing tool for jumpstarting recollection and introspection, at least for me. I wondered how long I'd been ignoring the clerks, uncomfortably seated in a semi-circle facing me.

Back to *Kerplunk* and the no-name tax case. I got the discussion going again and the youngsters gave me their thoughts. They were passionate about the issues and arguments, far more than I. It was a good reminder that even these stupid cases mattered to somebody. When they finished, or at least emptied their glasses, they adjourned to their individual desks, piled high with briefs and law books, and I packed my briefcase for home. Tomorrow, we'd do it all over again.

On Friday, we took our seats around the heavy antique dark wood table, well over a hundred years old, in our conference room. In front of me was a blotter, legal pad, and name plate, the latter another of the chief justice's ridiculous ideas. There were only nine of us. We sat in the exact same chair at the same spot at the table. When the membership of the court changed, we would shift a whopping one seat in order of seniority. Not exactly challenging to keep track of. I knew my own name, and none of us had reached the level of senility yet where we couldn't remember the other eight.

Justice Harry Cashman, my name plate read. They were little different than what you might find in front of a bank teller. Harry was my real name; not the more formal Harold which I was mistakenly called on a regular basis. It really didn't bother me, much less than it did in my youth, and was more of an irritant now, like a kernel from corn on the cob stuck between two teeth. I checked a mental box when I heard or read it these days; points off for the speaker or writer.

Chief Justice David Palmetto settled into his larger more ornate chair at the head of the table. His long stringy gray hair was over the collar of his robin's egg blue suit coat, more visually shocking set off as it was by the purple dress shirt and bright yellow polka dot tie. My rep tie, white shirt, wrinkled as it was, and dark blue suit looked positively antiquarian compared to his deportment. I sometimes ironed the front of the shirt, but never the back. He opened his leather portfolio to the preparatory notes it contained, like the college professor he was. He'd long ago figured out we didn't enjoy being lectured to, but could not break some of these longstanding affectations.

When appointed five years ago, he had installed a smart board on the wall of the conference room without discussing it with any of us. It was his intention to lead the conference discussion as he had his classroom at Yale. He was promptly disabused of this notion by the scathing memos he received from each sitting justice, yours truly included. Early in the term, like now, it was connected, somehow, to the internet and streamed a baseball game, the volume muted, or failing that, *Sportscenter.* This was a use of modern technology we could tolerate.

I sat on the far side of the table, on the side closest to the door, with Romo and Justice Perry Jacobs, two of the most disparate personalities on the court. Romo had short, dark hair, was a bit heavy set, but confided before the term started that she was committed to losing thirty pounds before we ended next June. I felt bad for her clerks this term who would likely miss out on the incredible Italian food she regularly brought to her chambers to feed "the children" as she called them. She was a strict Catholic, and highly conservative on most issues.

In the seat closest to the door sat the court's current junior justice, Perry Jacobs in an ill-fitting light gray suit, his shirt collar strangling his thick neck, if there actually was one there between his shoulders and head. The lighting reflected off his gleaming shaved skull. His clothing issues were not because he was heavy. Well, he was, but it was all muscle; Perry having played five years at linebacker in the NFL before law school. That background had helped during a raucous confirmation to his seat as he was also the first openly gay justice and as liberal as Romo was conservative.

Perry retained a few of the traits I assumed were helpful to him on the gridiron. Among these was his verbosity and ability to get into the opponent's head. Trash talking was not common in the judiciary.

"Come on, Chiefy baby, let's roll here. I've got a hot date tonight, a hunk from the Department of Agriculture." I bit my tongue to avoid laughing.

"Please Justice Jacobs, could we observe some decorum here. Remember where you are," the Chief Justice responded.

"Decorum, is that why you're dressed like a 14th Street pimp or a wide receiver?"

The chief put his hand to his head, now fully off his game.

"Some of the brothers I played with would like that suit. Hey I like the Mets in this game," Perry said, turning to our smartboard. "I'll lay fifty bucks on them. Anybody want in?

Yankee fan Romo leaned forward. "I'll take that action. The Mets bullpen sucks and this kid they have starting usually can't get past the fifth."

"You're on, baby. Too bad we have these cases to discuss."

"Please, ladies and gentlemen, some decorum. I too would like to get through our business expeditiously as I am attending the State Dinner tonight for the President of Botswana," the chief said, trying to regain control.

Our liberal gay football player and conservative Brooklyn Italian Catholic were, few knew, close friends off the bench. In opinions and during oral argument, they beat the living hell out of one another, through verbal and written jousting matches so vehement at times that some in the press believed the two despised each other. Just more evidence of the inaccuracy of the media.

Week one was too early in the term to turn the chief justice into a quivering lump of jelly, which Romo and Perry had done a few times during the previous one. The chief put on his airs in public but in our conference room, he was not a strong leader. That didn't mean the comedy routine put on by the two was appreciated by all the brethren.

"We certainly wouldn't want you to be late for what I am sure will be a riveting evening," Romo said, letting him off easily, her sarcasm evident to about half the group, which did not include the chief.

"Yes, well, let's begin with *Kerplunk v Forest* and the cast of thousands," the chief said, trying to be humorous. He did it about once per conference. "Bringing a little jocularity to the group," he described these so-called jokes.

"I'm generally of the opinion that the 9th Circuit overreached here based on *Cummins*..." his lecture began. We spoke and voted in order of seniority, the Chief Justice automatically being senior regardless of appointment date. Lectures at Yale Law were forty-five minutes in length, so we knew that was how long it would take him to review the case in detail and give us his conclusion. The senior associate justice would go next, although with a significantly shorter exposition, and so on.

Fifteen minutes after the chief had concluded his lecture, it was my turn to speak.

"I believe the circuit court overreached and would tentatively vote to reverse, dependent upon the logic used in the opinion," I said, making it clear, I hoped, that I had no interest in writing on the case. What I didn't say was if Kerplunk won, within a week, somebody would trademark "kerchoo" and "pfft," the sounds for sneeze and fart, and within a few weeks become the richest person in the world. Look out Elon Musk, Bill Gates, and Jeff Bezos.

It came out 6-3 to reverse. Romo and Perry split on the case, as expected, but neither seemed to feel it was worth giving blood over.

The tax case was even easier. Even the chief couldn't muster enough material for his normal lecture, concluding in just twenty minutes, for which we were all grateful. The outcome on that one was unanimous. The other cases argued this first week were similarly uncontroversial and looked like they'd also be unanimous or nearly so. A few easy ones to break in the new clerks in various chambers.

We then turned to the requests for cert on the docket. There were four that had made it onto the discussion list. A couple hundred had been received and reviewed by the clerks since the long conference in September, and these four had either caught the eye of one or more clerks or, less likely, one of the justices themselves. Cases that didn't make it onto the list for us to talk about in conference were automatically denied, although the parties to those would never know that their disputes, so incredibly important to them, never even received two minutes of our attention as a group.

The first up was another of the seemingly endless transgender cases. We had, I thought, disposed of what I called "the bathroom cases" but the states were always coming up with inventive ways to create conflicts which ended up on our desks. In this case, Mississippi had passed a law requiring that voters register as the biological sex they were born. It was unclear to me why the state even cared what sex a voter was to begin with, but the state legislators there obviously did, and with the 5th Circuit overturning the Southern District of Mississippi who had reversed the state, we were about to discuss it.

Thankfully, the chief's practice on cert petitions was to let the clerk's memo serve as the basis of discussion rather than subject us to an additional monologue by him. After introducing the case, he noted his inclination was to grant the petition. I wasn't surprised, as he had written extensively in the "bathroom cases." What surprised me was that he offered no indication as to which way he leaned.

Justice Judd Quackenbush, the senior associate justice, weighed in next, his deep baritone filling the room. When I closed my eyes, he reminded me of an old-time radio announcer. Quack was a swing vote, like myself. When we agreed, we were almost always in the majority. Appointed from the DC Circuit by Bush-the-second, he was as much a disappointment to his president as I was to mine. Beyond that, we had little in common. Married to his first wife for fifty years, he viewed my personal life with a jaundiced eye.

"This is a conflict within a single circuit that affects few people in a single state. I don't believe it warrants the attention of the court," he said. I put him down in my notes as deny.

When it got to me, there was still only one vote to take the case.

"Deny," I said without elaboration. The chief looked at me expectantly, but I said nothing more, looking down and pretending to write in my notes.

Romo spoke next. "I would reverse without argument. We've told the lower courts to stay out of state elections unless it's egregious. Failing that, I would vote to take the case so we can hopefully put these to bed once and for all."

I wasn't surprised, but her vote was what I feared. When it got to Perry, the junior justice and last to speak, there were three votes to take the case. I knew it was all over before he opened his mouth.

"Grant," said Perry. "You bet your sweet, well, insert body part here that I want to hear this one." I had no doubt he and Romo would have some interesting exchanges. Maybe, I thought, I would start a new game when we heard the case.

A week later, I sat in a large overstuffed leather chair in my chambers reading briefs for the arguments scheduled for early November. A stack of about thirty sat on a round antique table next to the chair, a rainbow of file folders. Blue was used for the petitioner, red the respondent, light green for amicus briefs on one side, dark green on the other. It was a helpful system. These thirty were not for the month, they were for a single case, a non-controversial one at that. Unless you consider reading until your eyeballs dried out difficult, I didn't consider it all that hard, hearing and deciding about seventy or so cases per term.

There were three sharp raps on the door which opened immediately. Justice Louis "Firewater" Freehawk stuck his head in. Firewater was the first full blooded American Indian appointed to the court. Justices had no problems getting past my doberman in the outer office. Anyone else had to worry, though.

"Have you heard the news?" he asked from the doorway.

"What news?" That apparently was his invitation to enter and he closed the door firmly behind him. Firewater was one of those opposite style nicknames, like "Slim" for a fat guy. Firewater was a teetotaler and proud of it. He wished the 18th Amendment instituting Prohibition had never been repealed.

Firewater took the chair opposite me but said nothing. I waited but finally could hold back no longer, and let him win this apparent contest between us.

"What news?"

"It's a sad day, Harry," he said, shaking his head.

"Will you spit it out, Firewater? What the hell are you talking about?"

"We received word that Judd has passed away."

I sat back in my chair, stunned. As old as Judd Quackenbush was, and I thought he was approaching his 86th birthday, he seemed in good health.

"That's terrible. What a shame," I said.

"It gets worse."

"How does it get worse than dying?" I asked.

"Judd passed away 'in situ' shall we say in the apartment of a young, very young, female attorney from the Solicitor General's office."

"Oh. Well, I can see how that will certainly make it painful for his family, and particularly Beverly." Beverly was his wife. "On the other hand, I personally can't think of a better way to go," I said, unable to hide my grin.

"Stop it, Harry. This will drag the court's reputation through the mud once it hits the media."

"You mean like I have?"

Firewater was known to think less than kindly about some of the items which had appeared about me in the Washington gossip columns over the past few years.

"Now Harry, you're not married, and while I admit some of the things written about you have been less than dignified, well, it's been nothing like this."

"True, while I have always adhered to my wedding vows while legally bound, I've obviously not felt constrained by the 'till death do us part' portion, and when not encumbered by the presence of a wedding ring on my finger, see no prohibition in sampling from the buffet table."

Firewater swallowed hard, twice, before responding.

"As is your prerogative. I feel simply awful for Beverly in this case, however."

"The public revelation will, I'm sure, be embarrassing. We don't know what Beverly may have known or not known behind the scenes, however. Within a few hours after this comes out, you can be sure the Rockefeller comparisons will be flying."

"You can't think Beverly knew about his assignation with this young woman?"

"Why not? She's the same age as him. She may have figured, *I don't want it anymore*, so if it keeps him from waking me up for morning delight, what do I care. Remember, Louis," I used his given name to make sure I had his full attention. "Nobody knows what goes on in somebody else's marriage but the two people who are in it, and from personal experience I can tell you, not always then."

He shook his head.

"I still can't believe…"

"Doesn't matter and we'll probably never know. The next couple of weeks, hell, the entire term is about to be turned upside down."

"Yes, I'm sure Judd will lie in state here for the viewing, followed by the funeral—he was Catholic—and then figuring out what to do with the cases argued to date, opinions assigned to him; so many decisions to make."

"And the penultimate one you haven't mentioned over which we have no control," I added.

He looked at me expectantly. I couldn't believe he hadn't thought of it, consumed by the immediate issues and lewd aspects of the news that were so troubling to him.

"Who that crazy bitch in the White House nominates as his successor," I said.

2

As Firewater predicted, the circumstances of Judd's passing overshadowed his long, distinguished career. A few serious journalists attempted to focus on his years of service but were drowned out by those for whom the salacious ending was the story, possibly concluding with a paragraph or two discussing his jurisprudence, if the editor had room. The family kept the funeral proceedings decorous. The president was conveniently out of the country, but the vice president, the administration's designated funeral-goer was there. The veep spent so much time at such events it was rumored his motto was "you die I fly." Most of the cabinet also attended, though the solicitor general and the lawyers on her staff were conspicuously absent, not surprisingly.

The following week we had our first conference since Judd's passing. Since we were early in the term, there was only one case where we were 5-4 with Judd in the majority. We agreed to put this single case over for reargument during the next term. The single opinion he had been assigned in another case was reassigned to another justice in the majority. We knew there were upcoming cases in which a 4-4 deadlock was possible, even likely, but there was little we could do about those now.

When we were done, the conversation shifted to the same topic the media had moved on to—who the President would nominate to fill Judd's seat.

"What're your spies at the White House telling you, Chief?" Perry asked.

"Honestly, I've heard nothing," the chief justice said. "I only know what I read in the papers, and believe only ten percent of that."

"The problem is identifying which ten percent to believe," Romo said, and everyone around the table nodded.

The names being bandied about by the media talking heads were a potpourri of the legal profession. They ranged from prominent professors who had never sat on the bench at any level, like our illustrious chief justice, to federal and state judges at a variety of levels. About the only thing missing were part time justice-of-the-peace level jurists. One wondered how many of these were real and how many anonymously leaked their own name in a desperate attempt to elevate their stature or perhaps get a raise at their law school.

The wildcard in all this was the President herself. To date, her appointees to the district and circuit court levels had been, in my opinion, a less than illustrious group. This was not surprising to me considering the President's personality and other appointments.

Henrietta Rubin Doyle was the first female President of the United States. Her late husband had been a long serving senator from Indiana who died in office. The governor appointed Henrietta to finish her husband's term, assuming he would then run for the seat himself when she cooperatively vacated the office at the end. He was in for a rude surprise. After two years in office, Henrietta had antagonized most of her Senate colleagues to the point where they assumed that living with her was what killed her poor departed husband. She did, however, set records for bringing federal money into Indiana, endearing her to the electorate who promptly returned her to the Senate for a full six-year term, to the chagrin of the ambitious governor.

In another two years, she'd parlayed her faux Midwestern roots—she was Jewish native of New York—and the story of the tragic death of her husband, into the Democratic nomination for the Presidency. After a campaign described, on a kind day, as ruthless, she destroyed her Republican opponent, who carried only three states. Her cabinet was full of political hacks and yes-men and women. Filling Judd's seat would be her first chance at a nomination for our court.

By the following week, a few names believed to be real had leaked from the White House. The short list was frightening in its mediocrity.

Romo, Perry, and I sat at the small round table in my chambers perusing the *Washington Post* and *New York Times* articles on the purported candidates. Perry had his iPad open to the SCOTUS blog, reading their coverage as well. The three of us each sipped from our beverage of choice, all containing alcohol, I assure you.

"Judge Hickam Q. Snifedorfer holds a seat on the regularly overruled 7th Circuit where he has written a total of three, count 'em, three majority opinions in the four years he's served on that court. Prior to his appointment, he served as the legislative liaison in the office of the late Hiram Doyle. You think he might know where a few bodies are buried?" Romo paraphrased liberally from the front page of the *Post* in front of her.

"He's a graduate of the illustrious Valparaiso School of Law in Indiana. Looks like it only took him three times to pass the bar. He's been divorced twice and is now married to another former Doyle staffer, fifteen years his junior," Perry read from his iPad. Perry was a law school snob, having graduated from Yale.

"He likes younger women. You and he will get along great," he said to me.

Romo grinned and I shot both the finger.

"Judge Ahmed... something I can't pronounce from the Eastern District of Wisconsin is supposedly on the list. Most of the reports seem to think he's not a serious candidate; on the list mainly to demonstrate that a Muslim was considered as part of the process." We were back to Romo again.

"That would sure fuck up the court schedule if he had to pray five times a day," Perry added his commentary.

"No worries. Apparently, he's not an orthodox Muslim or whatever they call themselves." Romo had switched to the *Times*.

"Well, that's a weight off my mind," I said, rolling my eyes. "Who else do you have?"

"Judge Mario Rocco Stallone, supposedly a distant relative of the actor," she said.

"What actor?" I asked.

"Rambo, Rocky, that guy," Perry said. "Just what we need, another guinea."

Romo kicked him under the table.

"Where's this guy from?" I asked

"He's apparently a state supreme court judge in California. Nobody seems to know what his connection to the administration is. He doesn't check any boxes. The Italian seat is full," Perry said, receiving another kick for his trouble.

Perry started tapping the iPad again and scrolled through some other news before stopping.

"Breaking news on the possible nomination, they say. What could this be?" Romo slid over to his side of the table to read over his shoulder.

"Uh oh," Perry said.

"Holy shit," Romo added.

"Who is it?" I asked.

"Read it again," I said, holding my head in my hands.

"Sources close to the White House indicate that one of the candidates receiving a close vetting as a possible nominee to the Supreme Court is Judge Judith A. Cashman, a federal judge from the Middle District of Pennsylvania in Scranton. Judge Cashman is notable as she is the ex-wife of current Supreme Court Justice Harry F. Cashman," Romo read from Perry's iPad.

"What the hell does the F stand for?" Perry asked.

"How, why…?" I couldn't form complete sentences.

"All it says is that the president met Judge Cashman at a conference in Aspen while in the Senate, probably one of those Obama things, and was impressed," Romo said.

"Unlike some of those other candidates, this is so incredibly awful, it must be true," I said, recovering just enough brain power to string a few words together.

"I thought you got along with Judith?" Romo asked.

"Cmon, Judy's not a hack like the rest of those asshats on the list," Perry said.

"Judy's an excellent judge, and unquestionably the best candidate on the list, and if I weren't sitting here, I'd be thrilled for her. She was a great mother to our children and I'll be the first to admit that how well they've turned out is far more her influence than mine. As a parent I have nothing but good things to say about her. As a wife, well, that's a different story; and as a colleague on the court, you might as well just get a gun and shoot me now. Pick out a spot next to Judd."

"There's no reason to assume she'll be nominated. It could be nothing more than making sure a female candidate was considered," Perry said.

"Sure there is. There's a great reason to assume it will happen. Because it will completely ruin my life." Perhaps I'd had one too many cocktails.

Her age, at sixty, worked against her a bit. Presidents like to appoint young justices, mid-fifties tops, and forties better, to maximize the years they could serve and influence the court. My appointment in my mid-forties put me on track for William O. Douglas—type numbers, potentially more than thirty-six years, if I lived that long, and didn't decide to bail out early and go fishing; an option that looked really good right now. The other Douglas comparisons weren't as flattering, mainly having to do with his number of younger wives and reputation for never having seen a glass he didn't want to empty.

Even so, it became clear over the next two weeks that Judith wasn't just on the short list, she *was* the short list. Her interview with the President lasted three hours, according to the White House public calendar. The other two candidates were relegated to fifteen minutes each late one morning, and neither was invited to stay for lunch. Judith's concluded about five in the afternoon, following which she adjourned to the family quarters with the president for dinner. It was all over but the formal announcement.

Romo shared a cocktail with me in my chambers that Friday following our conference.

"Have you called her?" She asked.

"Of course not. I'm a sitting Supreme Court Justice. It would be improper for me to reach out to a candidate for the court."

"Well, aren't we high and mighty today. Okay, has she called you?"

"That's different. Unfortunately, yes."

"And?"

"And I offered her my sincere congratulations, or at least as sincere as I could manage—which wasn't very sincere—on what looks like her presumed nomination. I then immediately changed the subject to our children, which is generally the safest topic about which Judith and I converse."

"Did she bring the conversation back to the court?"

"Of course she did. Judith is not an easily distracted woman when she wants something."

Finally perceiving I had no desire to disclose the substance of our conversation, Romo changed the subject.

"I guess your kids are excited about the prospect of Judith being nominated?"

"You'd guess wrong then."

Romo tilted her head and raised one of her thick, dark eyebrows.

"Our children remember how much fun it is when Mommy and Daddy interact under the same roof. Granted, our building here is a bit larger than the two-story colonial we had in Pennsylvania and the brownstone here in DC, but the point is the same."

"Christ, Harry, it's not the same. You're not married here. We all disagree with each other about cases and still get along."

"You asked what the kids thought. I told you. If you think they're wrong, tell them, not me. I'll give you their numbers. I happen to agree with them, though. Anyhow, she'll still have to go through the confirmation process, which is no walk in the park for anyone today, no matter how much the President likes you. Maybe there's a skeleton in her closet I don't know about. We can only pray, or we could if I actually did that stuff."

"Oh, come on, there's no way they'll dig up dirt on Judith."

"Unfortunately, I think you're right. She's as clean as new morning snow. I remember her mentioning cheating on a spelling test in the third grade, but somehow, I don't think that will come up. Hell, half the committee will probably spend their time asking her about me."

The next morning, just before lunch, the president and Judith walked out of the Oval Office and over to a podium awash with microphones on the South Lawn. President Doyle strode briskly up to it and smiled at the press gaggle and television cameras. Judith stood a respectful five feet back and to the president's right, as I'm sure the handlers directed.

"After a long and thorough search looking at the best legal scholars and judicial minds throughout the country today, I am pleased to nominate Judge Judith Cashman to the position of associate justice of the Supreme Court." She went on to make Judith sound like a combination of Oliver Wendell Holmes, John Marshall, and Antonin Scalia, rolled into one. She emphasized Scalia's writing skills, not what he actually said; probably a good thing for a President with her politics.

Then it was Judith's turn. She approached the podium, looking less nervous than I had been at my nomination, and made her prepared remarks, thanking every legal influence in her life, except me, and then the ceremony was opened to the vultures. The first question was the one I expected.

"Do you think there will be any issues working on the same court with your ex-husband?"

Judith smiled. "I'm sure it will be fine. Harry and I remain good friends, speak regularly, and attend our children's events together."

Christ, she made it sound like we were going to school plays and Little League games together. The kids were both grown and married—or living with someone in the case of our son. Maybe he had learned a thing or two from the old man. Her answer was word for word what the handlers coached her on, I was sure.

"Have you spoken to Justice Cashman about your appointment?"

"Yes, he congratulated me when he learned I was being considered," Judith said, not mentioning that she called me, implying that it was I who contacted her.

"Did he offer you any advice?"

"Oh no, that wouldn't be appropriate for a sitting justice, regardless of our previous relationship, and Harry is meticulous in such matters."

I let out a deep breath and hit the off button on the remote, not able to watch the rest. I was sure I'd get a complete report from Romo and Perry later.

Her appointment might have garnered a scintilla less interest, I thought, if Judy had gone back to her maiden name. Justice Judith Bertolini would have been a little less exciting to write about, but she never did, for a few reasons. At the time we divorced, she was already professionally established as Judith Cashman, and it was easier for the kids if Mom and Dad had the same last name. Oh well.

The next week, Judith began making her rounds, visiting the offices of all the senators on the Judiciary Committee and then as many others as possible. It was and is a time-consuming process. A short meeting would last a half hour and a long one would consume the better part of two. With twenty-two senators on the Judiciary Committee alone, it made for a long couple of weeks. Ultimately, she met with eighty of the one hundred. The others were unavailable due to scheduling conflicts, officially at least. The real reason was they were considered almost sure votes against confirmation.

A handful of these were rabid conservatives, Romo's kind of folks; but some others had noted they didn't believe a district court judge had sufficient experience for the "jump" to the top court. They noted that no district judge had been elevated to the Supreme Court since 1923 when Edward Terry Sanford was nominated by President Warren Harding. Harding wasn't on anybody's top ten list as far as presidents go, and Sanford, they were quick to point out, wasn't exactly a household name among Supreme Court justices.

The experience reason was pure bullshit. If former professors who never sat on the bench at any level, like the current chief, renowned Justice Felix Frankfurter, or state court judges, like myself, could do the work, there was no reason a district court judge couldn't. That said, I wasn't complaining about any of those predisposed to vote no on whatever rationale.

The clerks and Edith were silent on the situation; uncomfortable, I think, to venture anything signaling either support or sympathy. They didn't know what to say, like when someone is diagnosed with a chronic illness or fatal disease, perhaps a harsh comparison for Judith. The brethren showed no such reticence, with widely varying opinions, not unlike our cases. Some sympathized with me and others were enthusiastic about the choice with a couple in the middle, but not overtly opposed. The whole thing sucked. I didn't want Judy here, but at the same time, would feel horrible for her if she was rejected by the Senate.

As the confirmation hearings began, I became fodder for the late-night television hosts in their monologues; admittedly a self-serving view as many of the jokes were also at Judith's expense, but I didn't feel charitable. Looking back, I can admit there were a few pretty good ones.

As expected, a number of the questions at the confirmation hearings related to me. A few exchanges brought some laughter from those in attendance, along with Perry and Romo watching from my chambers.

The senior senator from Texas was a known no vote. He was also known to finish off a quart of Jim Beam before lunch. None of his colleagues on this or any other committee or subcommittee on which he served ever asked for a glass of water from the pitcher strategically positioned in front of him, as it was inevitably filled with vodka.

"In *Throckmorton v. Jones,* Justice Cashman wrote that it was okay for the hippie liberals of the EPA to protect turtles here in Texas. Now I don't know about you, but I happen to love me some good turtle soup, and there's plenty of the damn critters wandering around, so I just think this is another example of judicial legislating. How do you feel about turtles, Judge?" There were titters throughout the room, bringing glares from the senator and a rap of the gavel from the chairman. The senator had butchered what I'm sure was supposed to be a serious question prepared by his staff. Judith handled it well.

"Senator, I think a close reading would show that decision relates to the authority of the EPA to protect a single type of small turtle, not large enough for soup, that was in danger of extinction. It was narrowly written and since similar topics can come before the court it would be improper for me to comment further," Judy answered.

"You go, girl," Perry yelled at the television in my chambers.

"I dissented on that one. I wonder what he was supposed to ask?" Romo gave me a dirty look.

A senator from deep in the Bible Belt closed out the first day of questioning with this beauty, unquestionably referring to yours truly in his deep southern drawl.

"Judge, do you believe there should be a law or regulation limiting the number of marriages a justice can have?"

"Yes, Senator, I do, and there already is one. One spouse at a time has been the law of the land for many years." The senator from Utah seated next to the chairman turned bright red and the laughter throughout the hearing room was raucous, as the chairman decided to exercise his discretion to adjourn for the day instead of prolonging the agony. I tipped my glass toward the television in silent salute to Judy. Well played.

Less than a month after she stood on the South Lawn with the president and after clearing the Judiciary Committee on a 15-7 vote, the full Senate took up the nomination. Romo, Perry, and I watched the proceedings on C-SPAN. The final speeches concluded with the main advocates for, and the primary opponents against leading up to the roll call vote. I watched for entertainment purposes much as I did NASCAR for the wrecks. The outcome was preordained, practically every senator having already announced their position. After twenty minutes of the Yeas and Nays and watching senators mill around on the chamber floor, slapping one another on the back, the presiding officer pounded the gavel and the clerk announced the results.

"Seventy-five having voted in the affirmative and twenty-four against, the motion to confirm is carried." One senator was absent. It was a better number of "yes" votes than I had received those many years before. The chief had already told us to expect the formal oath for Judith on Monday morning.

Romo and Perry were quieter than normal. I think they recognized that regardless of their friendship with me, Judith was now one of us and they would have to work with her like any other justice. They both rose to leave, not knowing what to say, so I did it for them, raising my glass in a toast.

"Let the fun begin."

3

On Monday morning, the justices, minus the chief who was preparing for the ceremony, gathered in the robing room. By the end of the morning, each of us, again excepting the chief, would have shifted our wooden lockers, reflecting the new seniority. The court staff would move our stuff and the name tags on the doors, while we watched Judy take the oath. Nobody could remember how or why it started. It was a dumb tradition, but the court was filled with them.

I walked into the courtroom to greet our kids, who were in town for the event. Neither were too happy about being pursued by paparazzi and Fox News—pretty much the same thing—to get comments about their parents.

Judith entered with the chief justice, not dressed as she'd been for the announcement or confirmation hearings in the expected conservative, austere manner. Today she wore a short skirt, high heels which accentuated her tight calves, and her long auburn hair loose and flowing the way I remembered it when we first met.

Perry walked in and saw me staring, and sidled up beside me. He clapped his hand on my shoulder and said out loud what I was thinking.

"Damn, she's hot."

After the brief ceremony, attended by the president, Judith spent the rest of the day moving into Judd's old chambers. Based on precedent, any of us could have claimed his set of rooms, again in order of seniority, but I suspect all the brethren, like myself, became comfortable where we'd originally settled. There were slight differences in space and certainly the view from the various chambers. For myself, I didn't have enough energy to go through the work of moving and resettling, even with all the resources the court could provide.

She also was, I'm sure, getting to know her clerks, left over from Judd. She wouldn't get to hire her own until next term. District court judges have a single clerk, and they are usually right out of law school and not ready for the Supreme Court.

    I waited until around 5:30 to make my visit to the new justice, mine inherently a bit different than the others, the rest of the brethren not having shared a bed with their new colleague in the past.

    "Hello Judy," I said, interrupting her reading a brief, looking tiny behind the monstrous wooden desk Judd had used. A banker's light illuminated the center of the aircraft carrier sized blotter in the center of the dark mahogany, and another fifty to sixty multi-colored folders were piled to her left.

    "Hi Harry, I wondered if I'd see you today," she said.

    "It's tradition to pay a call on the new justice. You know I'm a stickler for such things, Judy, always have been."

    "Cut the shit, Harry," she said laughing.

    "Now Judy, while I may be less than fastidious about some of the social proprieties, the court's business is different," I said with an air of faux indignation.

    "Okay, Harry, I'll buy that since all the other justices have been by as well. I thought you'd be among the earlier folks. You know, get the pain over with, as it were."

    "Just saving the best for last," I smiled.

    "It's obvious my presence here has created some consternation among the court. There seem to be concerns by some of the justices as to how this impacts you. Nothing explicit, but it's hard to miss. Kind of sweet, in a way."

    "It's not about me, or you for that matter. The crap you read in the *Post* about justices not speaking or hating one another's guts is all fiction."

    "Until now?" She laughed.

    "We're talking right now, unless I missed something," I said.

    "A courtesy call, or a conversation about the kids isn't going to get it done when it comes to working together, Harry."

    "That's where you're wrong. You're not in Scranton anymore and we don't 'work together' up here. This is nine separate law firms under one roof. Our personal relations are good because we're professionals who can disagree agreeably. I don't go to other chambers for help on a case and others don't come to me. You're on your own here."

Judith stared back at me, absorbing the thought, looking like the proverbial deer in the headlights. It made me feel bad.

"Look, the work in the beginning is overwhelming. Shit, coming from the state court, I dealt with almost none of these issues before I got here. The reading will make your eyes fall out and the volume of it is why I practically lived in my chambers the first year."

"And I thought it was just to get away from me."

"Touche. All I'm saying is it's you and those four kids out there."

I walked over to the large globe in the center of Judd's, now Judith's chambers. "Do you want a drink?" I asked.

"I don't have anything, and none of the justices brought a house warming bottle," she chuckled at her joke.

I smiled and opened the globe. Hearing me drop two ice cubes into a glass, she laughed. I followed that up with three fingers of whiskey from the hand-cut faceted crystal decanter.

"Would you like one?" I reiterated.

"I'd love one, but no thanks. I have a lot of work to do, as you've so generously explained."

I raised my glass in a toast to her, and turned to exit.

"Wait, maybe I will have one. Is there anything other than whiskey in there?"

I turned back. "Vodka."

"A double, on the rocks. It's been a long day," she said.

She dropped the brief on the desk and took the long hike around the edifice while I poured her drink, and took a seat in one of a set of overstuffed leather arm chairs next to a round table. Even in the less than optimally lit room, I was again distracted by her legs as she kicked off her shoes, and tucked both legs under her, sideways. I handed her the glass of vodka, closer to a triple than double.

"Cheers," she said, downing a quarter of it. "Aaah, that's good. Are secret agent bars standard in every chamber?"

"Judd's, yours I should say, mine, and a couple others have something similar. Most don't."

"Well, I think that's one thing that can definitely stay," she said. "Tell me about the others?"

"I just did."

"The people, I mean, not their personal speakeasies."

"You've met them all," I said, a bit uncomfortable with the question.

"A handshake and 'welcome to the court' doesn't tell me anything and I certainly don't trust what I've read. After all, I've seen what they've written about you over the years."

"The good or the bad?" I laughed.

"I'm not sure I saw the good ones, but we'll let that go for now."

"You must not read the right newspaper," I joked. "No, there haven't been many good ones, especially over the last ten years or so."

"So, start with the chief justice," she said, her glass now half empty, and not letting go of the topic.

I sat back and took a sip of my own drink.

"Chief Justice David Palmetto is, well, pretty much that one law professor we all had who wanted to be liked but couldn't teach worth a damn. Thinks he's the second coming of Frankfurter but dresses like a pimp. At least Rehnquist earned the admiral's stripes he put on his robe by running an efficient court. Conferences with David are interminable. Writes his opinions more for the law reviews than the poor circuit and district courts who have to use them. Besides that, he's a decent guy."

"I got the impression he wants to be popular. I guess I can see how the opinions of one's former colleagues can carry some weight," Judith said. I stared at her over the top of my drink.

"News flash, baby, you're on the Supreme fucking Court of the United States and here for life. I don't give a shit who likes or doesn't like my opinions. The founders set it up that way for a reason."

She took another long sip, reflected on that, and unrolled those long legs from beneath her to rise and turn to the globe for a refill. Two clinks of ice later and a long gurgle of vodka, she sat back down and pulled her legs back under her, but the opposite way. I continued.

"Justice Louis "Firewater" Freehawk; you won't find a globe, at least like this one, in his chambers. If he could find four other votes, he'd reinstitute Prohibition. He's far from your stereotypical American Indian. I suspect the damage he's seen from alcohol in the Indian communities influenced him. He likes to gossip and know everybody's business. He's pretty much a nice guy."

"That explains why he wondered if you'd been in to see me yet."

"I'm sure that was his first question. Word to the wise. Don't refer to the Commanders as the Commanders. Unlike his Native American brothers, Firewater was royally pissed when the Redskins changed their name. If you go into his chambers on a Friday during football season, he'll almost certainly be wearing his legacy Redskins John Riggins jersey over his shirt and tie. He thinks it's good luck, although their record the last couple years doesn't bear that out," I said.

Judy laughed. "That's advice I think I can remember."

"Jose Cohen is a mongrel mess. He checked two boxes for his president filling both the Hispanic and Jewish seat with one pick. He's a great cook and you haven't lived until you've tasted his Kosher tacos."

Judy laughed a little louder this time, the vodka starting to take effect.

"Perry Jacobs is a walking contradiction. A gay former NFL linebacker, he usually has at least two hunks from one or another federal agency on his string. He enjoys messing with the chief's head immensely, and he and Romo—polar opposites judicially—are the best comedy act in D.C., except nobody gets to see it but us."

"Is he a top or bottom?" Judy asked.

"Excuse me?" The whiskey came out of my nose.

"You heard me."

"How would I know?"

"Harry, dear, I'm not impugning your manhood for Christ's sake. I better than anyone here know you're entirely heterosexual. I'm just curious."

"I have no idea, and as much as I like Perry, that falls into the category of too much information for me. You want to know, you ask him."

"I just might," she said, an evil drunk smile on her face.

I refilled my glass. I needed one after that.

"Antonia Romaldini, or Romo to us, is the Mutt to his Jeff or Jekyll to his Hyde. Shit, none of them are right. Anyhow, it's fun watching them make the chief stutter in conference."

"Is she...?"

"Romo's straight, although like with most unmarried women of her age, around this town there are rumors. Just unlucky in love, I guess."

"It happens."

"She's constantly on one diet or another, convinced it will make her more attractive. Bad for us, as she's the best cook on the bench."

Judy just nodded.

"Romona Henry is another matter. She's deep in the closet, mainly afraid her fellow mad-dog fundamentalist Christian conservatives would disapprove. She makes sure she hits a couple of the White House state dinners each year with a male escort—usually some desperate lawyer from one agency or another who's also fighting rumors—to tamp down the talk, but it's all for show."

"She sounds very conflicted."

"Romona is a sweetheart. She's serious about the work but doesn't take anything personally."

"Do the others?"

"Not much. The chief is probably the most sensitive, but he's concerned about his legacy and how history will judge the 'Palmetto Court.' We really have a pretty good group here. The novel writers, as I call the press, would have the public believe we're at each other's throats with every 5-4 decision that comes down and this one isn't speaking to that one, all bullshit."

"One of the first to stop by was Olivia Livingstone," she said.

"Olive Oyl is a wonderful old bird," I said.

"What did you call her?" The vodka splashed onto her blouse by her left nipple.

"She's as skinny as Popeye's girlfriend and has the same fingernails on the chalkboard voice, so I call her Olive Oyl."

"To her face?"

"Occasionally, particularly if I have a few of these in me," I held up my nearly empty glass and rose for a refill.

"She'll be the new senior associate justice now with Judd gone," I said.

"That leaves only one justice for you to tell me about."

"Who?" I counted them off on my fingers. I'd covered them all.

"Justice Harry Cashman."

4

"Right, well it's been a lovely visit and I hope you enjoy oral argument tomorrow," I said, rising to leave.

"C'mon, Harry, you've told me what every other justice is like. I don't know you here, haven't known you, really, in years. We talk about the kids and exchange Christmas cards. I want to hear it."

I stopped, turned, and sat back down. I'd definitely had too much to drink if she was making sense.

"Justice Harry Cashman, now second in seniority, where do I begin? Womanizer, a drunk, lousy father, legislates from the bench, if you believe the *Washington Times* or Fox News. Regularly compared to William O. Douglas; not for his jurisprudence but for his ever-younger wives and alcohol intake, part of which I've proven tonight. How's that?"

"Complete bullshit, but I'll let the specifics go for now. It's interesting how you can describe the rest of the brethren—I guess I get to call them that now—explaining how wonderful each is, but don't or can't do the same for yourself."

I rose to leave again, meaning it this time, and smiled.

"Good evening, Justice Cashman. I look forward to seeing you in the robing room tomorrow."

The next morning, Judith looked a bit under the weather as each of us donned our robes. We all shook hands, and proceeded to take our places behind the bench, only ten minutes late, another near-record for the chief. I often wondered if he ran his classroom the same way, especially since his lectures to us in conference were precisely forty-five minutes.

He called the case. We were hearing only one today, since it somehow was deemed to be of such importance as to require two full hours of argument.

"This morning we will hear *Town of Waverly v. New York*. Mr. Remmick, no it's Remnick I see, counsel for the petitioners, you may begin."

Francis Remnick had a huge Supreme Court practice and argued multiple cases in front of the court every term. The chief looked at him like it was the first time he'd ever seen him. I saw Frank roll his eyes as he rose to begin.

"Thank you, Mr. Chief Justice, and may it please the court…" I looked down and began playing my current game. With two solid hours, I hoped to complete two levels, outrageously optimistic on my part, but that was my goal. Usually, counsel had at least a few minutes of uninterrupted speaking before the questions and verbal jousting from the bench began, so I was relaxed.

Frank got about three sentences in when I heard Judy interrupt from the far end of the bench.

"Can you clarify the composition of the group bringing this action? Were they restricted to the current New York side of the town or were all residents allowed to participate?"

I shook my head in disbelief. Her question went way down into the weeds, to the facts of the case, and we didn't deal with facts up here. All that stuff would've been handled at the district court, worst case, at the circuit level.

The case was, at least in my opinion, a yawner, but the media had turned it into the next coming of the Civil War. The Town of Waverly was split down the middle by the state border between New York and Pennsylvania. The state income tax in Pennsylvania was about 3% and in New York, it was triple or quadruple that. Since the residents didn't get any worse service on the Pennsylvania side of the line, except for more and larger potholes—I knew, I'd driven through Waverly in years past—those paying three or four times the income taxes were not overly happy. Hence, they were attempting to secede from New York and join the great Commonwealth of Pennsylvania.

New York argued that the border had been established back around the time of the Revolutionary War or even before, so the Waverly residents could just suck on it. The lawyers in Pennsylvania submitted their state's view in an amicus brief that took fifty pages to say they really didn't give a shit if the border moved or not since the additional take by their treasury wouldn't amount to a rounding error in the revenue stream, and the roads they'd get from the New York side were in better shape than theirs anyway. Realistically, I don't think New York cared much either; these people already having cost them more in legal fees than they'd get back in taxes for years, but it was the principle of the thing.

For my part, I saw the case as an easy one, siding with New York. Those people all knew what side of the line they were settling in when they moved there, so to try to move the line now seemed like sour grapes. More importantly, I wanted to preclude the possibility of a hundred similar cases across the country if we let this town secede. It wasn't worth giving blood over, and sticking with my goal for the term, I had no intention of writing anything on the case.

The chirping kept coming from the far end of the bench. I couldn't help looking up again, my eyes rolling. The overall volume of questions had gone down somewhat following the Scalia years and nobody expected it to go back to the times when questions were rare during oral, but Christ, Judy wouldn't shut up.

It was like needles under my fingernails, I suspect, because she used the same tone with counsel that she used on me when we were married. *Take that, you poor bastards,* I thought.

It continued for the entire two hours. When it mercifully came to an end, I returned to my chambers, and dropped my phone on the desk. I hadn't even completed one level due to the distractions from the new junior justice. Before I could even sit down, Leslie entered.

"Uh, Justice Cashman, there may be a few news articles tomorrow about the case argued today," she said.

"Of course there will be, always are," I said, confused at her stating the obvious.

"No sir, that's not what I mean, precisely. I happened to be seated next to the press section and from the comments I heard, there will likely be some coverage of you specifically, sir."

"Me? I didn't ask a single question."

"Yes sir, that was noted. It wasn't what you said, but what you didn't say. Um, a number of reporters will be discussing, uh, your body language as a commentary on the questions by the other Justice Cashman." She blurted out the explanation in obvious discomfort.

"You've got to be shitting me," I said, slumping into my leather desk chair.

"No sir, a few reporters seemed downright giddy about the story."

"Wonderful, just goddamn wonderful." I seldom used profanity in front of the clerks, but this was ridiculous. "Okay, thanks Leslie," I said, and she exited, thankful, I think, for my minimal eruption upon her delivery of the wonderful news.

She was so right. With few exceptions, my head shaking and eye rolling led the court coverage the next day. Even the normally serious reporters who typically focused on the legal details couldn't resist a mention or two. The *Washington Post, New York Times,* NPR, and SCOTUS Blog; practically every outlet was present and accounted for.

Thinking about it, I had a few choices. I could ignore it, the standard stoic court response, or have some fun. I decided on the latter. Picking up the phone, I called the court public information officer.

"Good morning, Veronica, how are you this marvelous morning?" I opened.

"Just wonderful, Justice Cashman. A touch busier than normal, as I'm sure you can imagine."

I liked Veronica. She had a sarcastic sense of humor, an asset in dealing with the vultures circling her office on a daily basis, looking for raw meat.

"Really, I wouldn't have guessed," I said. "Would you care to share a cup of coffee this morning and chat about what has increased your workload?"

She chuckled. "Always at your service, sir. I'm on my way."

I rang Edith and asked her to send in a pot of coffee, swiveled my chair toward the windows, and enjoyed the historic view.

In ten minutes, both Veronica and the coffee arrived. We sat at my small round table and sipped the strong brew.

"Do you have any preferences on how you would like to handle this?" After the routine pleasantries were disposed of, we got down to business.

"We could start by saying Madam Justice Cashman was instrumental in my failure to reach my goal of two additional levels on the game I was playing on my phone."

"And what game would that be?" She asked, taking the bait, her brow furrowed.

"Is that germane?"

"The media will think so."

"Do you think they would be surprised that a Justice is playing 'Hitman Go' on his cell phone during oral argument?" Veronica enjoyed video games and we had talked about our favorites in the past.

"Surprised isn't the first word that comes to mind," she said, burying her head in her hands.

"What word comes to mind?"

"To be honest, impeachment was the first. There were others but I keep coming back to that."

"My, that does seem harsh. Perhaps we should try another approach."

"Yes, I think that would be advisable," she said.

"Why don't you just say, then, that Mr. Justice Cashman has long made his personal preference clear that counsel should be allowed to present their arguments without an inordinate number of questions from the bench. That opinion has not changed and he has no comment on the perceptions of the media gallery. Then you can add that you happen to know that the Justice has been recovering from a head cold, which may have impeded his normally intensive note taking during the oral argument in question."

Veronica smiled for the first time since entering my chambers.

"I like it. We're stuck with the story for a news cycle no matter what, but it will die a natural death after that with this statement. Assuming two things…"

"What are those?"

"That you don't die an unnatural death the next time you see the other Justice Cashman…"

"And the second?"

"That tomorrow you stick to your game and don't look up."

The following day, we heard argument again. I was tempted to send one of my clerks for a set of those bright yellow moldable ear plugs, but I suspected they might be noticeable from the press seats. Instead, I doubled down and increased my concentration on killing people on my phone; transference, the psychologists reading this will infer. It worked, and there were no subsequent articles about my body language, and I completed one level in my game. I directed Leslie to locate a source of flesh colored ear plugs, however, as a precaution.

Our Friday conference, thankfully, put some limits on Judy's verbosity. As we discussed *Waverly v. New York,* I cast my vote with New York, unwilling to open the sluice gates to secession cases from every Podunk town near a state border who saw a lower tax rate on the other side. Judy, as the junior most justice, spoke and voted last, the outcome already determined. She threw her hat in with the dissenters, making it 5-4 against Waverly.

    I was, I thought, safely in the middle of the pack on the majority side; not rabidly for the state or only just barely. Someone holding the latter position was a common target to be assigned the opinion, thought to cement their vote with the majority. I was therefore surprised when the chief looked at me, practically glowing in the bright orange shirt and purple tie he wore, looking like an over-colored Easter egg.

    "How about you write this one, Harry?"

    Although phrased as a question, such assignments are not really requests, based on our long-standing traditions. I had been assigned only one opinion this term prior to Waverly, so with the normal practice of trying to balance the numbers between the justices, it shouldn't have been as much as surprise as it was. I nodded and made a quick note on my pad. The clerks, Leslie specifically as she was the lead on the case, would be thrilled. I wasn't. Then my day got worse.

    "Judith, would you please try your hand at a dissent, since we seem to share the same views on this?" Olive Oyl's squeaking, grating request was followed by a demure chuckle as she looked directly at me, an amused smile displaying her tea-stained teeth.

    Why you bitch, I thought. *Why don't you just bend me over the table and stick it in.*

    "Certainly Olive…I mean Olivia," Judy turned a bit red at the slip, as she too looked at me. Olive Oyl pretended not to hear and put a checkmark in her notes.

    I walked back to my chambers alone, not desiring any company, and waved the clerks into my office while passing Edith's desk. They followed me in as I dropped my leather portfolio on my desk, looking at me expectantly. There was no way I could muster any false enthusiasm.

    "We've got the Waverly opinion," I said.

    "Do you know who's dissenting?" Leslie asked.

    "As a matter of fact, I do," I said, settling into the soft leather tufts of my chair. Leslie continued to stare at me. Her eyes said "and?"

"Justice Cashman will be writing for at least herself and Justice Livingstone," I said.

The color came up in Leslie's face.

"No problem, sir. This opinion will be bulletproof. We'll kick her…"

"Leslie, gentlemen, we're not playing football here. This isn't a contact sport. We have a legal disagreement; this isn't personal."

"Yes sir, I understand. I'll get right to work on it."

"No rush, Leslie. I don't care if this doesn't come out until the June rush," I said. I noticed John nod with understanding. Obviously a perceptive and worldly young man.

"But why, sir? This case isn't complicated. We can have this ready to circulate in a couple weeks." Leslie either wasn't quite as bright as I'd originally thought, or was a bit more naïve.

"It might be best if Justice Cashman, the other one, uh, her first published opinion isn't a dissent from a majority by our Justice Cashman." John explained it perfectly. I nodded almost imperceptibly to the young man, like a mafia don.

Leslie looked at John, and then back at me. "Oh, I see, sir." The competitive expression was back on her face.

"Alright team, let's get back to work," I said, this time able to sound more enthusiastic than I felt.

I watched John and Leslie whispering to each other as they left. The other two were silent. I'd have to keep my eye on young John. He had the makings of a Pennsylvania politician.

We had another week of arguments before a short break for Thanksgiving and then another two before a longer recess for Christmas and the New Year. It wasn't a vacation for us. It was a scheduled period to work in a concentrated way on opinions; majorities, dissents, and concurrences, as well as prepare for the argument sittings still to come, and stay current with the never-ending stream of cert petitions. On the first day of the so-called break, there was a knock on the door and Judy entered after my acknowledgement.

"Do you have a minute?" she asked.

"Always for a fellow justice. What can I do for you?" I responded more cheerfully than I felt, dreading it was a court-related visit, rather than a question about what to get one of the kids for Christmas.

"I was wondering when you will be circulating your Waverly draft? I can't go any further with the dissent I'm writing until I have your opinion to respond to."

"Maybe you should wait to see what I've written before dissenting. Perhaps my indisputable legal rationale would persuade you as to the correctness of my view." I couldn't resist the tweak.

"You're wrong. The basic presumptions of our country; every precept of the founders demonstrate that these citizens should be allowed to affiliate with Pennsylvania. That line on the map is totally arbitrary."

I laughed. Her face grew red, and her eyes narrowed. The hurricane was spiraling up. I needed to explain.

"Judy, you need to save your passion for a case that really means something, not bullshit like this. I couldn't give less of a damn whether these fifty or however many people pay Pennsylvania or New York taxes. I do give a shit about not opening the door to fifty or more similar controversies that we'll have to decide if a few people in this whistle-stop town get their way."

"But..."

"And no, you won't read about any of that reasoning in my opinion which will be narrowly written on the facts and precedent which established this border well over 200 years ago and which will ignore your high-faluting Declaration of Independence crap which, in case you haven't noticed, does not have the force of law behind it."

"The nation's jurisprudence should not be decided on reasons or rationale which isn't public," she protested.

"You're not on the district court anymore, Judy. This is the big leagues. And to answer your original question, you'll get my draft opinion when I decide to circulate it, and not before. I'm not sure you get it, but I'm trying to do you a favor here."

"A favor, oh please explain," her voice dripped with sarcasm.

"Don't you think that on your first published opinion here, it would be nice if we're on the same side? Doesn't matter if it's a dissent or majority. I don't really care, but it might get us less coverage, not only in the legal press, but the gossip pages as well if it doesn't look like we started off fighting. Believe me, we'll have plenty of chances to disagree and be on opposite sides."

Judy looked at me, the understanding crossing her face. She now got that Olive Oyl was having some fun at both our expenses. She couldn't let the opportunity pass, though.

"Change your vote on Waverly, and that can happen next week," she said, turning on her high heel and marching those shapely legs out the door.

I adjourned to my bar and poured three fingers of scotch into a tumbler and added a handful of ice cubes. Kicking back in my chair, I raised first one, then a second unpolished shoe to the corner of my desk and stared at the bookshelves stacked with bound decisions of the court, dating all the way back to *Marbury v Madison,* and even beyond. If reflection is good for the soul and scotch is good for reflection, it therefore must follow that scotch is good for the soul, temperance fanatics like Louis be damned.

With the first drink winding its way to the neurons of my brain, I rose and strode back to the bar, refilling my glass with both the amber liquid ambrosia and ice. Returning to the desk, I hit the buzzer for the clerks, and asked them to come in. It was past the end of the regulation work day, but they were all still present and accounted for, workaholism a common clerk trait. They didn't know how easy they'd had it to this point of the term.

Entering as a group, they headed toward their usual seats. I interrupted before they reached them.

"It's cocktail hour, boys and girls, so please join me with your choice of libation." I gestured toward the open bar with its liquor, seldom used mixers, ice, and glasses. They looked at each other nervously, and then John, my future politician, took the plunge, mixing himself a seven and seven. A plebian drink, to be sure, but one in which at least the alcohol could be tasted. The other three followed, Leslie pouring herself two fingers of my best scotch, neat. I was impressed. From the choices, it appeared we were down to a single teetotaler in the group, a good sign.

"I've called you here for this chat to explain a few things," I began after they'd taken their seats and a sip or two of the drinks each held, serious looks on their young faces. I wondered if they expected me to announce my retirement. If so, they were in for quite a surprise.

"You may have noticed that your work load, in comparison with your fellow clerks in the other chambers, has been less. Your justice has, until now, consciously avoided writing dissents or concurrences and only reluctantly taken on the assigned majority opinions." A pretentious formulation, *your justice,* I thought; probably fueled by the liquor. No matter, I proceeded.

"My reasons for this are personal, but I will share with you that I have felt a reduced enthusiasm for the court's work since my recent divorce. This has abated, and the remainder of the term will be entirely different. I intend to lay out my views on our cases whenever and wherever I think they add to the legal discourse on an issue. Therefore, you can all expect to get much busier. Are there any questions?"

"I have one, sir." Leslie took a large swig in preparation. "Do you plan to write on any of the cases currently outstanding?"

I frowned and took a sip of my drink.

"That's an excellent question." Leslie beamed at the compliment. "I haven't really given it much thought. Adding a bunch of dissents or concurrences to opinions already being circulated, while not unheard of, would certainly toss a hand grenade into the conference. Let me consider it over the weekend. There may be something that comes out that I just can't abide, and that would certainly cause me to write. But what I'm aiming at are the cases to be argued between now and the end of the term."

There were no more follow up questions.

"Have a refill if you like," I said, which they correctly interpreted to understand that our meeting was over. After they left, I refilled my glass, switching to club soda, and settled back behind my desk, wanting to be clearheaded while I enjoyed the twilight view out the window. I looked forward to the next round of oral arguments for the first time in a while.

5

The new week of arguments started where the previous left off, Judy chirping away on the far end of the bench, and me with a newly engrossing game on my phone—I decided to take a break from killing people for a bit. The case was a no-brainer in my mind, one we took to slap the hands of a rabidly conservative three judge panel in the 5th Circuit.

The police in Austin, Texas knew they had a drug dealer operating on the 8th floor of a local high-rise, but couldn't make a case against him. Someone in the department got the bright idea to fly a drone with a camera up to his windows and peer in. Seeing drugs on the kitchen table, they declared them to be in plain sight, busted in the door, and arrested the dealer. No warrant for the drone, the entry, or anything.

The 5th circuit agreed with the cops completely, reversing the district court which had thrown the case out on its ass where it belonged. We took the obvious Fourth Amendment violation to put an end to this crap before it became pervasive, or so I thought.

Judy relentlessly questioned counsel for the drug dealer with one hypothetical after another about plain view, all designed to elicit agreement with what seemed to be her theory that height was irrelevant to plain view. I found her hypo about the airline pilot seeing marijuana growing on a roof top garden particularly amusing. Based on the perspiration droplets on the lawyer's broad forehead, I assumed he did not share my enjoyment.

The chief tried to move the argument on with little success. I tried to focus on my game.

"So, you would not agree a pilot flying a police helicopter over a backyard garden seeing marijuana cultivation, at five hundred feet elevation, could direct reinforcements, as it were, to apprehend the grower whom he observed watering his or her crops?" Judy further refined her pilot hypothetical.

"Justice Cashman, we see myriad search and seizure issues with such a situation, and those are beyond the potential practical ones, such as the ability of a pilot to distinguish marijuana plants from other herbal growth at such a distance," the lawyer wiped his brow with a handkerchief.

"If I might join the conversation for a moment," Perry boomed into his microphone, glancing sideways at Judith, who finally shut up for a few moments. "Would you stipulate that had the police obtained a warrant to utilize the drone, having presented sufficient probable cause that your client would be processing narcotics, that we wouldn't be here having this hypothetical tour de force?"

"In general, yes, I would agree with that, Justice Jacobs."

Perry's question made it clear how he would be voting, trying to send a not-so-subtle message to Judy. She would have none of it. Her hypothetical marathon continued when the state began presenting. The Texas attorney general, making his first appearance before the court, was thrilled to take her questions.

"Mr. Ewing, can you comment on my police helicopter observing marijuana cultivation while on patrol?"

"We would not differentiate between that and an officer on street patrol observing a drug transaction, Justice Cashman," he said. "Height is not a factor, ma'am." His twang was as thick as the cow manure he was spreading. I looked up.

"And the fact that the helicopter observation is completely accidental and the drone a purposeful, planned, operational intrusion into a private residence doesn't trouble your logic?" I asked, almost assuredly buying myself another newspaper article, or ten, for the next day, but I couldn't resist.

"Uh, no, Justice Cashman, sir, we don't believe there was an intrusion."

I smiled and sat back and watched Romo take over, having put cheese in the trap.

"We've ruled that the use of infrared cameras without a warrant is not permitted. How is flying eighty feet in the air and sticking a GoPro up to a window any different?"

"Because the narcotics were in plain view, Justice Romaldini. The infrared camera couldn't confirm the presence of drugs, only infer it from the heat signature.

"I don't think I buy your distinction, since hypothetically, the occupant could have been a baking enthusiast, and the bags of white powder your camera saw, confectionary sugar and flour," Romo made her position clear.

I risked a surreptitious glance at Judy. Her face was blank, trying to appear indifferent. She now understood she was distinctly in the minority on this one.

I redirected my attention to my game for the balance of the argument, trying to get a level completed, looking up only when the chief intoned, "the case is submitted."

The discussion of the case at conference on Friday went quickly after we concluded the chief's forty-five-minute lecture. It was eight to nothing when it got to Judy. As I expected, she stuck to her guns, giving a lucid but unconvincing five-minute argument that the use of drone cameras without a warrant to visually search a residence should be an allowable Fourth Amendment exception. There was polite acknowledgment at the conclusion.

"Don't worry, dear. We all end up alone in dissent on some cases," Olive Oyl advised.

"Indeed, Judith, staying true to one's principle and a healthy debate is valuable to the court and country." I hoped the chief would stop there. I'd heard the remainder of this speech at least a half dozen times. Luckily, he was interrupted by Perry.

"You go, girl," was his sage advice. I held my tongue. It was the last case of the meeting, so we rose to leave. I made my way back to my chambers, not noticing until I reached the doorway that the chief was almost alongside me.

"Would you have a moment, Harry?" he asked, as I opened the door.

"Certainly, David, come on in," I said. Edith was surprised to see the chief justice follow me into my office, but said nothing.

I put my leather portfolio down on my desk, and held my hand out to the chairs around my table. The chief took a seat, and I took the chair opposite him.

"What can I do for you, David?"

"Based on the past Fourth Amendment decisions you've written, I had it in mind to assign the drone opinion to you, Harry, but with the, shall we say, unusual voting outcome, wanted to discuss it with you first."

I tried not to smile.

"Pay it no mind, David. We're all going to have to get used to this and I had planned to voice my interest in the opinion." I had no such plan, but this was too good to pass up.

"Splendid then, it's yours," he said, rising to leave. We shook hands, and he departed.

I hit the buzzer on my desk. "Edith, please ask the clerks to join me." The bar was my next stop. Ice cubes and two fingers of Jim Beam seemed appropriate. The clerks entered, and I motioned to the bar. They replicated their drinks from last week, and settled in around the desk.

"We have the drone opinion," I said, sipping the cool, amber liquid, which immediately turned to golden warmth inside me. "This one is yours, John, if memory serves."

"Yes, sir," he said. "Any guidance beyond the disposition discussed in the bench memo?"

"None. It should be a straightforward opinion. You should know, though, that it was not unanimous, as I had thought it would be. Eight to one; close but no cigar."

"Who is in dissent?" John asked.

"Justice Cashman," I said, chugging the remainder of my drink to hide my smile. The grin on John's face matched the one my glass hid.

An hour later, I still sat at my desk, jotting down a few phrases for John to include in the draft, sipping my third drink, when there was a knock on the door.

"Come," I said, and not surprisingly, Judith entered.

"Pour yourself a drink," I said, and she proceeded directly to the bar, which did surprise me. After getting her drink, she took one of the leather chairs across from my desk.

"Did I make a fool of myself today?" she asked.

"Depends on your objective," I said, not in the mood to be conciliatory.

"I'm convinced my position is constitutionally correct."

"You're entitled to that opinion based on nomination by the president and the advice and consent of the Senate. Eight of us, also nominated and confirmed, think otherwise. Means we win." My blood alcohol was probably too high to have this discussion.

"Well, isn't that a mature outlook," she said.

"Have a couple more of those, and maybe it will make sense," I said.

"Touche," she answered, raising her glass.

"Look, there's one very important rule around here. A famous old Irishman once used his hand to demonstrate it. Five fingers, you can do anything around here with five votes, he said. You can try to make it as intellectual as you'd like, the way our nutty professor chief justice tries to, but it doesn't change the fundamentals, and five, any five of us, can do pretty much whatever we want. Now getting to five, that's another discussion."

"I'm not stupid, Harry. I've heard the Justice Brennan stories." She used the same tone she had used when telling me to pick up my underwear or take out the garbage. It sent shivers down my spine.

"It's the rare justice who hasn't been alone in dissent at some point during their time on the court. I've been there a few times, and could be again tomorrow. That's the beauty of the lifetime appointment. Doesn't matter if anyone agrees with you, including me."

She drained her glass and rose.

"It scares me when you make more sense drunk than you do sober, Harry."

"Maybe I should start writing my opinions at night, then," I said.

"Or drinking during the day," she laughed.

"Don't tempt me."

I stared at her tight red blouse, the second button undone, and the well-shaped calves accentuated by her high heels. Shake it off, I told myself. I should be thinking about that new blonde civil rights division attorney I met the other night at the French Embassy party. Mid-thirties, no kids, just my type. We'd exchanged texts twice since then. Just enough to demonstrate interest but not so much as to appear desperate. Dinner on Saturday night; that would be perfect. A nice Italian place I knew. I reached for my cell phone and hit her number.

"You bastard," she said, barging into my chambers without even a knock. The clerks were stunned, our Monday morning discussion of upcoming cases interrupted by Judith's unexpected entrance.

"Come on, Judy, tell me how you really feel," I said.

She was silent for a moment, surprised and embarrassed, not expecting anyone else to be present. It didn't last long.

"Would you please excuse us? Justice Cashman and I have something important to discuss," she said, steel in her voice. The clerks scattered like flushed white-tailed deer in a Pennsylvania forest.

"You bastard," she repeated when the last clerk disappeared through the door.

"I believe we've already covered your opinion of my lineage," I said. "Care for a drink?"

"No, I don't want a drink. It's nine in the morning. Stop trying to distract me, you son of a bitch."

I rose to get myself a cup of coffee, from the pot Edith had left earlier, raising one eyebrow at Judy. She reddened slightly; with the understanding I had not been referring to an early morning visit to my globe.

"Given a choice, I think I'll stick with your initial term of endearment, if you don't mind," I said. Her face grew redder.

"You knew on Friday you had the opinion in the drone case," she clenched her fists like she wanted to use them. The chief's assignment sheet had come out bright and early this morning.

"The chief confidentially discussed his desire to assign it to me after conference, but nothing is official until formally assigned."

"Don't use that tone with me, you bastard."

"Well at least we're back to that. Look, have a beverage, and sit down and if you won't do that, at least take a few deep breaths."

Her color lightened, fists unclenched, and she walked to the bar, morning hour be damned.

"I haven't drunk this much since...I don't know when," she said, pouring herself a short vodka.

"Welcome to Washington."

She slammed it back and then sat down. The red-hot anger dissipated.

"Why didn't you tell me, Harry?"

"What good would it have done?"

"We could have discussed the case in more detail, rationally."

"No, we couldn't have. You don't change anybody's mind around here like that. We've all been doing this for a while. I change my mind due to oral argument or from our conference discussions maybe once per term, sometimes not that much. And a written opinion makes me switch my vote less often than that. But let's hypothetically say that your incredible powers of persuasion got me to change my mind. It's still seven to two, babe. You still lose."

"Is that what this is about, winning or losing?"

"Not at all. While it's nice to be on the so-called winning side, I really don't give a damn one way or another in the vast majority of these cases. Do you think I give a shit about some obscure tax code provision from 1952? My job is to apply the law and interpret the statute or constitution as I see it. If four others see it the same way, great. If nobody else does, I'm fine with that too."

"I made my position clear with my questions during oral argument," she said.

"Oh, you certainly did."

"You don't approve?"

"It's not up to me to approve or disapprove. We've had this conversation. Each of us are independent entities who arrived here by ourselves. I've made my opinion well known over the years that I think there are too many questions during oral. Let the lawyers have time to get out a sentence or two uninterrupted. This isn't supposed to be law school where we're professors who hammer the students through the Socratic method."

"I like the dialogue with counsel. I think it helps clarify things."

"Like I said, suit yourself. I would gently remind you that you're not in the district court anymore where you're the only judge on the bench, though. Nobody has said you can't ask questions, but you have plenty of company up there who like too as well. You might give them a chance to get a word in edgewise too."

"You obviously pay attention to my questions. You're over there, head buried, taking notes like mad throughout the argument."

I laughed, spilling my coffee on my blotter.

"What's so goddamn funny?"

"I'm playing video games on my phone," I said.

"You're doing what?"

"You heard me. I got two levels completed during the drone argument."

"You son of a bitch."

"Are we back to that? I much more enjoyed being a bastard."

6

Dinner on Saturday night had been enjoyable. The young lady was a delightful companion. Intelligent, articulate, beautiful, she was everything I like in a woman. Under ordinary circumstances she would be an excellent choice for a prime spot in the rotation of candidates to be the next Mrs. Cashman. That is if there were other candidates, and if I were looking for the next Mrs. Cashman. It didn't feel like ordinary circumstances, though. Maybe it was my age, the recentness of the divorce, my reinvigorated interest in the work at the court. I wasn't sure. There was another possibility, but I refused to consider it.

Late Tuesday afternoon, Judith paid another visit to my chambers, entering without the thunder and lightning of the day before. We spent fifteen minutes going at each other, hammer and tongs, over the meaning of the word "that" in a small subsection of one clause of the bankruptcy code. It was the type of case which made up the largest percentage of our docket, but which would receive next to no news coverage; it wasn't sexy or controversial.

"I don't understand why you're all fired up about this. Olive Oyl is writing the opinion," I said.

"Wouldn't it be nice to be on the same side in a case, Harry?"

"We are on the same side. I'm concurring with the opinion. I agree with the result, just not how she got there with her interpretation of the clause. The damn case is unanimous, for all intents and purposes. Even Romo agrees, although she's writing a concurrence as well. She has a third interpretation." I could tell she was exasperated.

"How was your date?" She asked. This conversation was starting to resemble ping pong.

"Fine," I answered, figuring I had either ended up in one of the society page "sightings" columns again or she had already established an intelligence network in town rivaling the CIA. The odds were even.

She whacked the ball back to me again. "Do you want to come over for Thanksgiving dinner?" Thanksgiving was Thursday, I immediately realized.

"Sure," I said, without thinking. Then it hit me.

"Hey, I didn't think either of the kids were going to be in town this year," I said.

"They're not," she said, opening the door to leave, her light blue high heels clicking on the hard floor, the color matching the blouse she wore.

"You can bring the wine," she said and the door clicked closed.

The court was recessed for the week of Thanksgiving. That didn't mean we weren't working, just that no arguments or conferences were scheduled. It increased the perception among the public that being a justice was a part-time job. The court calendar was not our friend in that regard.

After Judy left, I went back to the first drafts of Leslie's work on Waverly and John's on the drone case. The two clerks were brilliant lawyers. They were also young, and not Supreme Court Justices. The two drafts would go through upwards of a half dozen revisions each before I would consider circulating them generally.

On Wednesday morning, John and I spent the morning talking through my comments on the drone opinion draft.

"It's too long. Cut at least a third out of it, maybe half. We're going to categorically dismiss the argument that height doesn't matter. You don't have to spend eleven pages repeating all the counter arguments. Let the dissent do that. Also pick the five most relevant cases, cite those, and then you can say there are dozens of others. I don't want to waste paper saying we've got thirty cases to your two, therefore we win. That's not how it works."

"Yes sir," he said, brow furrowed.

"Spit it out, John,"

"Well, sir, it's just that, well, when I clerked at the circuit court, we were instructed to…"

"You're not at the circuit court anymore. The best way to send a message to the lower court that they got this totally wrong is a short opinion. Shows the judges that not only was the circuit wrong, they were so wrong the Supreme Court only took ten pages to tell them so. This isn't a nuanced case where it could take a dozen pages to parse precedent and arguments."

"Yes sir, that makes sense, I guess."

"Easy to say, hard to do. The opinion has to be crisp, polished, totally devoid of anything unnecessary. We're lawyers. It's in our blood to write long. That's why I've edited the hell out of this. Don't worry, we'll still have to add to it once the dissent comes out, but our comments on that will be short too. You don't have to respond in detail on an 8-1 opinion. Let's sit down again early next week and see where you are with it."

The rest of the day was spent with Leslie reviewing the Waverly draft. It was going to be a longer opinion, there being no on point precedent to point to—on either side. That meant a more complicated narrative to explain why the history, case law, and constitution required this result. Even so, I didn't want it book length. She'd done a good job laying the foundation. Now we had to make the language mine.

In the warm fall temperatures we experienced in DC, Leslie wore a fashionably short skirt, her legs bare, and surprisingly tan based on the calendar, with medium high heels. Not as toned as Judith's, her extremities were still distracting as she crossed and uncrossed them during our discussions. It made me wonder about fraternization among the clerks for just a moment, but I'd seen no signs of such activities.

Even with the necessary complexity, there were sections of the opinion I thought could be condensed and tightened up. Such thoughts were as antithetical to Leslie as they'd been to John.

"My favorite briefs," I tried to explain, "are the ones that are shorter than the permitted page limit. That tells me the lawyer said what he or she needed to and then stopped. Most think that if they don't use every allowable page, their client isn't getting their money's worth and, I guarantee you, there are clients who feel that way. There are lawyers who believe their work on the case is so important, so vital, that if we gave them double the page limit, they would use it. That we should be deprived of even a scintilla of their brilliance horrifies them."

Leslie nodded. From her expression, I could tell she was mentally dividing the briefs she'd read into the categories I described. I continued.

"My way is far from the only way, and not necessarily even the right way. All you have to do is read the opinions coming out of some other chambers in this court to see that. Some justices insist on responding to everything in the petitioner and respondent arguments, the dissent, if there is one, and some of the myriad briefs. It's no wonder we're running out of shelf space for the printed volumes."

"I appreciate you explaining this, Justice Cashman. It just seemed there were so many compelling arguments that needed answering," she said.

"True, and you will find that in many cases here. That's why, some of them at least, are on our docket. But I'll leave you with one thought on how I've come to write opinions. We tell them why we're right, not concentrate on why they're wrong."

Leslie nodded, pursed her lips, uncrossed her tan legs, and headed for the door. After she left, I sat back and thought about how many times I'd given that same talk to a clerk. Maybe someday I'd convince one of them.

My arms were full when I reached the door of Judith's condo. She'd bought a place in a nice building, a nicer place than mine. DC real estate isn't cheap. I suspected she'd sunk over a million into it.

Two bottles of wine, one of good bourbon, and a bouquet of flowers filled my arms. I'd thought about picking up a box of candy, but that seemed rather fifteen-ish. It made it challenging to reach the doorbell, but I succeeded.

The door opened and she greeted me in another one of those outfits designed to show off those incredible legs. The skirt was much shorter than anything she would wear to the court. I'd have gone ballistic if my daughter wore it.

"Wow." It was all I could manage.

"Thank you, kind sir," she said in a faux southern accent, doing a partial curtsey. Anything more was impossible in that skirt.

I put my contribution to the meal on the counter and she looked at the bottles, making approving noises. She glanced at the flowers and smiled.

"I think I have a vase around here somewhere," she said. It was apparent that while she didn't dislike the flowers, the wine and booze were higher on her scale. I was relieved I had discarded the candy idea.

An incredible smell filled my nose. My olfactory senses joined forces with my memory trying to place the wonderful mellifluous odors coming from the kitchen. Then it hit me; our kitchen in the house we'd shared in Pennsylvania, and the Thanksgiving dinners Judy had cooked back then. I was amazed how a simple smell could create the warm feelings washing over me.

"That smells incredible," I said, closing my eyes and raising my nose to take it in deeper. Judy laughed. I opened my eyes to see the head-shaking smirk she offered.

"It's turkey, Harry. You had it every year when we were married. I can't believe you haven't had turkey for Thanksgiving since then," she said.

"Uh, neither of your successors were much for home cooking. You don't get the same experience in a restaurant," I offered, a lame excuse to be sure. Judy gracefully ducked the opening I'd given her to comment on wives two and three.

"Why don't you open these bottles and pour us a taste while I check on the bird," she said. I was happy to have a change of subject and a task. I opened the lovely Burgundy from a good year and producer and a terrific lightly oaked California chardonnay. The chardonnay was already chilled, having spent the last twenty-four hours in my refrigerator.

We tried both wines; the bourbon having been set aside for later. Not having the ability to translate taste into the descriptive berry-laden wording of professional wine critics, I'll simply say both were outstanding. The smell from the kitchen got even better, if that was possible, after Judy removed the turkey from the oven to rest on the cutting board while she finished the mashed potatoes and gravy. Added to the coleslaw, cranberry sauce, and rolls, it was the classic Thanksgiving dinner of earlier years.

"Would you carve the turkey, Harry?" Judy asked, and with a glass of each wine already under my belt, I happily took up my labors.

We sat down to eat, Judy with an apron of the type my grandmother wore, protecting her expensive dress against spills. The wine and food were magical, taking me back years. Much better than the fare at any five-star restaurant where I'd partaken of holiday meals in the recent past.

Over dinner we talked about the kids, most of which I won't repeat here. We did discuss when one of them might first make us grandparents, which I will mention on the off chance they actually decide to read this. Consider it a hint.

For dessert, Judy produced a fresh-baked pumpkin pie from the kitchen, and I broke out the bourbon I'd brought. A few sips of the smooth liquid gold combined with the luscious pie and the tryptophan from the turkey had me more relaxed than I'd been in years. I thought about classically loosening my belt a notch, but discarded the idea as a bit dated.

We called each of the kids to wish them happy Thanksgiving, ignoring the surprise in each of their voices that mom and dad were celebrating it together without one or both of their presence.

Adjourning to the couch in the living room, Judy carried a tray with coffee and cognac to the low table in front of us. With the football game playing on the television, sound muted, we savored the beverages, both spreading warmth throughout us, or at least me.

After the second brandy, the comfort of the surroundings won out. The next thing I knew, I awoke on a couch in the dark, shoeless, and covered with a quilt. My mind went to work in an expedited fashion to determine my location. The speed of these calculations was necessitated by the full bladder which was the cause of my awakening, and the immediate need to do something about it. Working through the possible permutations, I correctly concluded I was on Judith's couch. Now I needed to remember where she told me the damn bathroom was.

After locating it and solving the urgent problem of the full bladder, I had another decision to make. Did I slip my shoes on and drive home through the empty DC streets with an unknown blood alcohol content, an easy target for any Metropolitan police officer bored on patrol, or return to the auspices of the comfortable couch? For an instant, I considered the option of slipping into what I assumed would be the more comfortable bed that Judy was in, correctly eliminating that option as dangerous on many possible levels, including being smothered with a pillow by an angry ex-wife upon discovery.

Having calculated the low odds of reaching home without a detour through at least a breathalyzer exam and possibly the city DUI processing center and city lock-up, I returned to the couch, covered up and returned to my slumber. I woke up again as the sun began to glow in the living room windows. Judy was still asleep so I started the coffee maker, already set up to produce a full pot. I made myself a to-go cup, slipped my coat on, and closed the door quietly as I exited.

I drove home through the quiet streets. The only crowds this morning, known widely as Black Friday to Christmas shoppers, were at malls and other retail outlets, none of which were on my route. At home, I took a quick shower, shaved, and changed clothes. With nothing on my schedule for the day, I decided to go into the court for a while.

Not having extensive experience in early morning departures from a female's living quarters, I left a simple note saying "thanks for a great night, talk to you later" on top of Judy's coffee cup, next to the full pot, minus the one cup I took before leaving. I didn't want to wake here, but didn't want to leave without communicating, either. I was well outside my comfort zone on the proper etiquette for such a situation, but had little doubt I would receive remedial instruction before the day was out if my effort was deemed incorrect.

I walked into my office in a surprisingly good mood. That was aided by no residual effects from the wine and other beverages we consumed last night. The building was almost empty other than the ever-present court police and a skeleton maintenance staff.

The only other car in the area reserved for the justice's vehicles was Romo's. Edith and the clerks were enjoying a four-day weekend, as were the rest of the brethren, apparently.

I decided to read through some cert petitions. These were from the pile of those set to be discussed at our next conference. Even the small percentage of cases that made it that far was winnowed much further. It was almost to the point that buying a lottery ticket had better odds than getting one of the seventy or so formal arguments in front of the nine of us.

Picking up the first folder, the case name itself created no inherent interest. What was inside, though, hit like a double espresso to the system. *Brown v IRS* involved the tax collection agency being sued by Brown over a determination by someone at a high desk wearing a green eyeshade in the bowels of the IRS building that Brown's product line, at least some of it, was subject to a special medical device tax. Brown argued that the government, in its never-ending thirst for additional revenue, had grossly miscategorized certain products they manufactured and sold. Sex toys such as vibrators, dildos, and other named items I, thankfully, was unfamiliar with, were listed as medical devices that the IRS was taxing, apparently with the concurrence of the highly conservative Fifth Circuit. If anyone else had been in the room,

I strongly suspect they would have seen my eyes roll. I could hear the questions from the bench already.

Some of my colleagues would be completely confused, and no amount of input from the briefs or discussions with young, and far more worldly clerks, would educate them, or me for that matter. Others would be red faced and utterly silent. Then there was Perry. If there was one vote to take this case, it would be his.

I could hear him questioning the IRS lawyer now. "Can you explain how the agency made the determination that ben wa balls are a medical device? In my personal experience, while I understand there's pleasure from their use, I know of no therapeutic value that would justify the categorization and tax." Jesus.

There was no question that Brown was getting screwed by the IRS, pardon the pun, but this unique dispute was not something we should be spending our time on. I put the file in my deny pile. There was no way we'd get away without Perry insisting on putting it over for more than one conference. The enjoyment he would get from discussing it would be palpable. The red faces he would produce, particularly on Olive Oyl and Firewater, would entertain him immensely. The relisting from conference to conference would get the attention of the court media, but no one else, thankfully, and after milking the enjoyment out of it for a month or so, he would let it go. At least it would be amusing.

The next folder was for a case I would take for the pure joy of making my local postmaster squirm. *Clutterbuck v USPS* argued a hard to dispute point that the postal service was incompetent. If you couldn't put an envelope with an address on it in the correct mail box then you needed to think about a remedial reading class or another job. The petition argued that the management tolerating this level of incompetence should pay the people who sent the envelopes, as well as those who didn't receive them. The district court had agreed with this rationale, but the circuit court, with a more detached view, or better letter carriers, had unanimously reversed. As both my mail carrier and postmaster were serial offenders in this area, I could envision myriad punitive findings to work into an opinion. No clerk would so much as touch a draft of this one in my chambers. Sadly, I doubted anyone other than me would see the case as something we should take, and unlike Perry, I wouldn't have it put over for weeks just for my own amusement. Well, maybe for one week, I would.

My private line in the office rang. I picked it up assuming it was one of the kids, or a telemarketer concerned about my auto warranty. Judy's voice came through the ear piece.

"Why in the world are you at work? I called your cell, but it went right to voice mail so I took a chance."

"It was this or join the throngs at the suburban malls for the Black Friday sales," I said.

"Funny. You're making me feel guilty I'm not in chambers, especially being so new."

Now I felt bad. There was no reason for me to be here, but I understood why, as a new justice, she would feel that way. I tried to think of a way to explain to her that I was here because I had no real life, especially following the divorce, without seeming pathetic. I wasn't here because I thought the work demanded it. Before I could muster my thoughts in any sort of coherent manner, she changed the subject.

"What are you doing tomorrow night?"

"Nothing," I said, without thinking. While I had enjoyed my dinner with the young lawyer a week or so ago, I had not followed up on any future dates, and there were no other candidates on the docket.

"Let's go out for pizza like we used to," she said.

I was silent for a minute, trying to come up with a reason to decline. The more I thought about it, though, the wholesome attractiveness of such a simple evening grew on me.

"Okay, but I have no idea where we should go," I said.

"I'll do some checking on line. There must be some good pizza places in DC. I'll let you know tomorrow," she said.

We hung up and I sat back, confused. Why was I looking forward to tomorrow night?

Around seven the next evening, I found myself seated at a small table in a hole-in-the-wall old school pizzeria Judy found for us in northwest, for the uninitiated, one of the four quadrants of DC.

Tables lined the wall of the railroad car type space, each covered with a red and white checked table cloth. The lighting was dim, supplemented by candles in classic straw covered Chianti bottles on each table. An ancient dark oak bar ran the length of the restaurant opposite the tables and behind it at the far end were pizza ovens and a white-haired Italian man, with a flour covered shirt and apron, making pizza after pizza in full view of the customers.

The wine list was short, all Italian, and mainly Chianti with a few barbera's and moscato's mixed in. The beers were pedestrian, which is not to say bad. Fancy craft beers would have been out of place here, which seemed to have been lifted right out of the 1960s. The background music was from a jukebox in the corner, which appeared to be authentic to that era.

The Stegmaier we sipped from frosted beer mugs while looking over the one-page menu took me back to Pennsylvania. We ordered an extra-large eighteen-inch pizza with no toppings, and a middling level bottle of Chianti. Our waiter, almost as old as the pizza maker, nodded approvingly at the classic order, clicking his pen on the order pad he wrote it on.

I turned sideways, soaking up the atmosphere, watching the old guy twirl pizza dough. He made pizzas with machine-like efficiency, take out order boxes filled with pies covering the top of the double bank of ovens, staying warm.

Judy was enthralled as well. She fished in her purse, came out with some coins, and walked to the juke box. She perused the selections, dropped the coins in, and punched the white buttons on the front of the well-lit machine to add to the current playlist.

The waiter arrived at the table as she got back, pulled out her chair for her, and set the bottle and two glasses he carried in one hand on the table as he opened his cork screw. Removing the capsule, he pulled the cork, avoiding the pop that was the sign of an amateur. He poured a small taste in my glass and waited. I gave it a quick swirl, sniff, and sip, not expecting anything spectacular, and was pleasantly surprised, which the waiter saw from the look on my face. Smiling, he poured an inch in my glass, the same in Judy's and set the bottle on the table for us.

The pizza tossing wasn't for show. The old guy didn't even look at the customers, many of whom, like us, were fascinated. I guessed those that weren't paying attention were regulars.

A few minutes later, our massive steaming hot pizza arrived at the table. Paper thin, with an air bubble here and there, it was a picture-perfect New York style pie. We each slid a slice onto our plates, and sipped our wine, waiting for the near molten cheese to cool sufficiently not to burn off the roofs of our mouths.

"How'd you find this place?" I asked.

"Google, Harry. You should try it some time," Judy laughed.

Unable to resist the smell any longer, I picked up the slice, blew on the tip, and took a bite. Even near oven hot, using a knife and fork here would be blasphemous. Perfection was the only word I could think of; the sauce, cheese, and seasonings took me back thirty years or more. It was that long since I'd tasted pizza this good. I chewed, moaned, and took another, larger bite. Seeing that a trip to the burn unit was not in my immediate future, Judy took her first bite and a similar, but higher octave noise, emanated from her side of the table.

Our hunger and the incredible food overcame any desire for conversation until each of us had eaten two slices.

"This was a great idea," I said, sliding a third slice onto my plate between sips of the lovely Chianti.

"It's so good," Judy said.

"Why pizza?" I asked.

"I figured we could go to a place like this without ending up in the gossip pages like we would if we went to the Capitol Grille or someplace like that."

"Yeah, I'm convinced some of the hostesses and maître d's do a nice side business selling out their customers to the photogs and Washington version of paparazzi. Of course, I think it works both ways. Some of the customers probably slip them some cash to make sure they get their picture taken. There are politicians in this town who would knock over a woman carrying a baby to get their face in front of a camera."

"I just think the simple pleasures like this are relaxing, and I don't know about you, but I could use it," she said.

I laughed.

"You don't think so?" She asked.

"That's just it. I do. I don't think I've been this relaxed in the last two, three years," I said.

"Then we'll have to do this again," Judy said, eyeing the pie to decide if she could fit another piece into what I'm sure was a rather full stomach.

"Go ahead, live a little," I said.

The conversation changed to work, but the lighter side.

"Did the chief tell you about your two other jobs?" I asked.

"Other jobs? Isn't the one I have enough?" Judy asked.

"Traditionally, the junior justice is the door answerer, if that's a word, during our conference. A most important position. If somebody knocks on the door, you get up and open it. Perry could disagree with you on every decision we write the rest of the term and he would still be thrilled you are here because it means he no longer has to answer the door."

"I think I can handle that," she said, sipping her wine and picking up the slice she was working on.

"The second job is the head of the cafeteria committee, but you don't have to worry about that one," I said.

"Why?" She was genuinely curious.

"Because for some reason, the chief immerses himself in all cafeteria-related issues. I hear the staff there hates him. He writes endless memos on menu minutiae, most of which are useless."

"Most?"

"Well, there was one serious issue. Serious for me. Nobody else gave a shit."

"Do tell." She sat back with her glass, ready for the story.

"He organized a group of volunteer taste testers and proposed to replace my beloved Heinz with Hunt's ketchup."

"And what did you do?" She laughed, having been married to me and knowing my obsession with the Heinz brand. No other ketchup was permitted in our house.

"I wrote back, with copies to all the justices, that obviously the philistines he had doing the test had taste buds effected by long Covid and could not be relied upon. I told him if he followed through with the change, I would publicly release a dissent and organize a boycott of the French fry counter, if not the whole cafeteria."

Judy laughed. "And his response?"

"He backed down, of course. I knew he would not want to get involved with a public airing of a ketchup controversy, particularly with my Pennsylvania roots," I smiled. "I'll go along with certain things: stretching the Fourth Amendment here and there, some statutory interpretation differences, but don't screw with my Heinz ketchup," I said.

"Well, Harry, I'm glad to see some things haven't changed," she said, shaking her head.

We finished the bottle of wine, passed on what looked like amazing cannolis for dessert, and took home the couple remaining slices of pizza in a to-go box.

Judy climbed into my car. She had Ubered to the restaurant. It was a quiet ride to her condo, punctuated mostly by comments like "oh, I'm so full" from both of us. Arriving, I walked her through the parking garage and we went up the elevator, and took the short walk to her door. She found her keys in her purse, stuck them in the lock, and turned back to me.

"Thanks Harry, I had a nice night."

She kissed me on the cheek, turned, and entered the condo. The door closed. I turned to walk back to my car, touching the spot where she kissed me. I felt 16 years old again.

7

On Monday after Thanksgiving, during our short recess, I undertook one of the tasks I both anticipated and dreaded, each term. It was mundane, to be sure, but necessary. It was my annual interview day for clerks. I, we, all of us didn't simply hire for the next term. That would be far too simple. No, I would be interviewing kids for a slot to be one of my clerks for two or three years out.

I call them kids, but these were not brand-new lawyers fresh from law school and the bar exam. Before they ever reached us, most had spent one or more years clerking at the district court and then with a judge on one of the circuit courts. Most were a year or so north or south of thirty when they took one of the desks in my outer office.

Some would have had a year in a U.S. Attorney's office or a low-level justice department job. The more socially conscious would have spent time on a public defender's staff someplace. The resumes were damn near interchangeable, except for the names of the judges, districts, and circuits. They were supposed to be the best and the brightest; the Navy SEALS of young lawyers.

Most of us took recommendations from circuit court judges we knew and liked. Feeder judges, the media called them. Some only hired clerks from their alma mater. Some only from the circuit they were responsible for. There was no right or wrong way. I took a more unusual approach.

Reading through the resumes, I ignored the usual things one would look for. I paid no attention to their law school, grades, law review membership; these were all high-end and near perfect. I looked for something, anything, different. A kid who collected stamps, was a volunteer firefighter, a serious bass fisherman, tattoo artist; things like these would instantly attract my attention. Anybody who was something I wasn't got my attention. It might not get them the job, but could get them an interview.

Edith showed the first victim, or candidate, into my chambers. Trudy was a nice-looking young lady with medium-length light brown hair. She was dressed in standard interview-wear; a knee length skirt, high button blouse with a feminine blazer, and flat shoes.

Writers of descriptions of women's fashions have no worries of me taking one of their jobs. I took immediate notice of her hands when we shook, soft and well-manicured. After reading her resume, this surprised me.

"Have a seat." I motioned to one of the leather chairs at my small round table. She sat, demurely tucked her skirt tight, and looked at me expectantly.

I suspect my interview style varied from that of most of the other justices, although I was sure Perry had a unique methodology. The differences between the majority, Perry, and myself, was likely vast. I saw little sense wasting time on the cliché questions which would receive robotic pre-prepared answers. I started with whatever item got the candidate in that chair.

"Your hands are soft and well-manicured," I began. Her cheeks reddened as she glanced self-consciously down at her hands, now not knowing what to do with them.

"Do you do any of the mechanical work on your race car?" I followed up and she began to breathe again.

"Oh yes, Mr. Justice Cashman, all the time, or at least every chance I get. Last week I updated to a new Holly carburetor. I'm hoping for a few more horsepower." I suppose I looked confused while again looking at her hands. My grandfather had been a mechanic, and while none of his mechanical aptitude was genetically passed to me, I did remember that his hands were like leather covered in sandpaper. Smart young lady that she was, the lightbulb went on and she got the reason for my question.

"I wear nitrile gloves while working on the car. We all do. It's more to keep the parts clean than our hands, but I guess it does work out well in that way," she added.

Now I understood. Trudy, her resume showed, raced modifieds on Pennsylvania's dirt tracks on Saturday nights through the summer. Not something that showed up in the standard clerk resume, which is why she was here. We spent most of the allotted time with her teaching me about tire stagger, carburetors, and what it feels like to flip over in one of those cars. I'm sure she was quite confused by the time I ended our visit with the standard, "we'll be in touch" comment.

Candidate number two was Vance, a tall, thin young black man who spent part of his undergraduate time as an Ivy League champion pole vaulter. Track and field is far from my favorite sport, but if it comes on during channel surfing *and* if the pole-vaulting event is on, I watch with rapt fascination. The speed, proper placement of the pole, how severely it bends, and the ride to the top and hopefully over the bar placed at a ridiculous height, captivates me. As with Trudy, Vance's academic achievements, clerking assignments, etc. after graduating from Princeton were stellar.

Following the ritual handshake and seating, like Trudy, my first question went directly to the most important item in my mind based on his impressive resume. It was most definitely not one related to a particular area of case law or constitutional issue.

"How do they make those poles so they catapult you over the bar without breaking?"

I then sat back and listened to a concise fifteen-minute history of the evolution of the technology of the pole, starting with solid ash, then bamboo, and the path to aluminum, fiberglass composite, and now carbon fiber. Similar to my practice at oral argument, I did not interrupt, happy to listen to someone so well versed on the subject; one which he was obviously passionate about. It also showed his ability to take an obscure technical topic and make it understandable to the average person; a valuable skill to a clerk, advocate, or Supreme Court justice. It was a fascinating journey through the history of the most important piece of equipment in the sport, and the new knowledge would greatly enhance my enjoyment the next time the pole vaulters came on my television screen.

The third, and final, contestant for the day entered my chambers about a half hour after Vance departed, and the eclectic interest education program for intellectually curious justices continued. Julia was a Penn State Dickinson law graduate—I tried to give the Third Circuit schools some love in selecting clerks. Her judges were among the stellar list that successfully fed me good clerks over the years. Like Trudy and Vance, though, she was here for another reason.

During her high school and undergraduate college years, Julia spent what appeared to be an extensive amount of time as a firefighter and emergency medical technician. As one who jumped every time I lit the grill and queasy when bandaging a paper cut, I was fascinated by the three-sentence blurb from her resume describing her training and experience in this area.

I changed up my approach to the initial question with her, going more open ended and quasi-legal, but making clear what got her in the door.

'Has your experience going to emergencies and the like had any effect on your work in your clerkships, legal views and so on?" I hoped this would allow me to delve into the nitty gritty of wearing the coat, helmet, and air tank, and deciding when to blow the siren. How many fires have you gone to, etc.? Obviously, all critical questions for a young lawyer looking to clerk for a Justice.

My questions elicited fascinating stories about fires and accidents, but as with Vance and Trudy, the technical minutiae fascinated me.

"The coat, pants, boots, helmet, and breathing apparatus weigh about 45 pounds. When you add the radio, flashlight, thermal imager, and miscellaneous hand tools that each of us carry, you can easily have around 75 pounds on your body," she informed me. To be able to walk, much less function effectively carrying that much weight was astounding. Learning that fire apparatus, as she called the vehicles, could cost over a million dollars each, especially the ladder trucks with two drivers, made my jaw drop. I would have a new appreciation as a taxpayer the next time I drove past a firehouse and saw the truck being washed and cared for.

Our first case back after the recess was a snoozer. We were hearing a water case. They weren't unusual and becoming more common, especially from the south and west. Because reservoirs, rivers, creeks, and aquifers span multiple states, conflict over use of these resources was inevitable. The district court usually appointed a master to go through the facts and tell the judge, who had a bit more expertise than I did, but not much, what to do.

In this case, one southern state was pissed that citizens from another southern state were taking too much water, or so they contended, from the aquifer via their wells. I guessed the pissed off state thought the other state's folks were taking excessively long showers or something. The only good thing for us is we are supposed to assume the lower courts got the facts right and just deal with whether they interpreted the law correctly. The bad news is, in just about all of these lately, the appeal was based on the lower court not following the law correctly because they got the facts wrong.

It was a good case for me to make a couple levels in the game I was working on. The phone was fired up and I was doing good. Perry asked a question which I didn't pay any attention to. Then he went off on a riff.

"Are you saying without saying that we should overrule *Rickover v. Arizona*?" A case the lawyer hadn't even mentioned.

"Because if you have a persuasive argument there, we would need to revisit virtually a century of other precedents." Perry did this once, sometimes twice a term. A Neil Peart drum solo of legal thought. A soaring crescendo of legal theory and philosophy. I looked up to see the lawyer's face. A litany of changes occurred, going from attentive to confused, to near terror, trying to follow the path of brilliant tortured logic coming at him. Perry had stopped talking to the lawyer by now, his face looking up, speaking toward the ornate ceiling. Finally finished, and returning to the standard rock beat, he looked down at the lawyer, and back and forth on the bench, ready to let the rest of the band continue the song.

Having seen this before, Romo came to the advocate's rescue.

"Let's move on," she began an entirely different area of questioning, letting him know Perry's snare, tom, and cymbal virtuoso was rhetorical and needed no response. The lawyer looked like he would kiss Romo the second his time concluded. I went back to my game.

The last case of the week was one I had looked forward to. Not because of any exceptional constitutional issue being at stake. The motivations were admittedly base, perhaps even childish. It was about watching a large number of states beat up on a single one. A state that, perhaps, had it coming based on how much of an economic bully they had become. Highly restrictive emission standards, product labeling requirements, and the ironic if not downright amusing cutoff date for selling gasoline powered vehicles. The absurdity of a push toward electric cars needing regular charging in a state that couldn't keep the lights on for an entire summer was ironic.

In this case, the attorneys general in twenty-five states, both red and blue, sued California for the smoke from forest fires which traveled east and degraded the air quality in the plaintiffs states multiple times each year. The air quality numbers in each during those times exceeded acceptable levels of both state and federal regulations.

They could have come right here, since the court had "original jurisdiction." The founders set it up that way so if one state thought another state wasn't playing nice, it was one of the few situations they could come straight to 1st Street, NE, our building. They hadn't in this case, for various tactical reasons, but they were in front of us now.

California had tried to get the case dismissed, then tried to have it relocated to a "friendlier" district in California, also knowing they would have the receptive 9th Circuit in their back pocket upon appeal. They lost on dismissal and transfer, then lost at the district and circuit court levels in both the 2nd and 3rd circuits. Apparently, east coast judges liked clean air too.

Based on the decisions to date, California was going to have to raise state taxes by upwards of thirty percent, the proceeds of which would be entirely dedicated to funding additional forest fire fighting capabilities and capacity. The federal government had told them they weren't getting another thin dime on top of the millions the U.S. Forest Service already spent each year on wildfires there. The state of California had been told to keep your smoke to yourself.

The states used a quiver full of arguments, ranging from air quality number violations to due process. California looked silly saying that restricting smoke was the same thing as restricting interstate commerce. The attorney general from Michigan gleefully asked in response why did his car factories have to add special emissions equipment to sell a car in California? Oral argument was, for once, amusing enough that I barely looked at the game I was working on.

The discussion on Friday at conference surprised me a bit, when after the chief's lecture, I was the first vote against California. As it turned out, the chief and Olive Oyl were the only votes *for* California, making me the senior justice in the majority.

This had happened a few times in the past, but with Judd's passing, and my move up the board, as it were, such an occurrence was more likely going forward. I knew that Perry had a particular interest in the case, but it presented a more enticing opportunity, one I knew he would understand. Once the count became clear, I looked down the table, past Perry.

"Judy, would you take this opinion for us?" I asked.

Her eyes opened wide with surprise. Perry looked at me, some confusion on his face at first, but then the lightbulb went on and he grinned at me.

"Certainly, Harry," Judy said, making some notes on the pad in front of her.

On Monday, an emergency petition landed on my desk from the Third Circuit, the one assigned to me. The volume of these had increased exponentially during the Roberts Court era. We had tamped that down some, but still saw more than we should. Emergency was in the eye of the beholder.

In the usual scenario, a district court judge slapped an agency or department over a policy or action brought before them by someone disgruntled over the result. The judge wouldn't just apply it to that case or their own little world, but would make the order or injunction nationwide. The agency or department would be pissed, but instead of waiting for the circuit court to hear and resolve the issue, they would appeal directly to us. Yes, even presidents have been known to employ this gambit—I don't need to tell anyone who the most prominent practitioner of these appeals was.

Very few of these were real emergencies. I disliked what I thought was overstepping by the district court judges as well as the lack of patience of the agency or department. We had three main options in handling these. We could grant the request, overturning the district judge, almost never done. I could refer the petition to the full court to see what the brethren thought. They could grant, turn it down, or decide to hear the case on an expedited basis. Or I could do what I did in ninety five percent of these cases which was deny it myself without referring it to the full court. I had done so many of these, I had a template which only required me to write in the case information and send it to the printer to get it issued. It's a little more complicated than a single paragraph makes it out to be, but this covers most of the options and avoids me having to burden you with a footnote. More on those later.

Emergency grants by the full court seldom resulted in "good" decisions. The record wasn't fully developed, as it would be if it went through the normal process and was heard by the circuit court before us, and these were usually emotional issues. I looked over this one for about three minutes, thought about how I wished I could find against both the district judge and agency, and then denied the case with my handy dandy form.

    The Christmas holidays were around the corner. I was writing in a half dozen cases; majorities, dissents, concurrences, which kept the clerks plenty busy. Christmas day was on a Thursday, so because of work schedules, the kids were coming to town the weekend before to celebrate with Judy and I, and then would spend the holiday itself with their significant others and associated families, all of which were near where they both lived.

    We met at Judy's on Saturday to exchange gifts with them. They both wanted to see their mom's condo. We had a nice dinner, if expensive, at Charlie Palmer's, and then reconvened on Sunday morning for breakfast before they left for their respective homes.

    A good time was had by all. It was apparent they were watching to see if there was increased tension between Judy and I with our new working arrangements. They left satisfied that things were fine.

    I hung around for another cup of coffee after they left, planning to spend the afternoon in front of my television set with a couple of football games. Judy bustled around the kitchen, cleaning up the detritus from breakfast.

    "What are you doing for Christmas?" she asked, while loading plates into the dishwasher.

    I hadn't really thought about the actual day. Whatever day I saw the kids constituted the holiday for me.

    "No idea," I said, adding a little more creamer. Apparently, I was too used to Edith's tea water coffee.

    "Why don't you come over here Christmas Eve and I'll cook us a nice dinner?" She asked.

    "Sure," I said, quietly pleased with the invitation.

    The football games were just okay; I couldn't get overly excited watching my teams lose. The take-out pizza I had delivered less so, especially after what we ate the night of our "pizza date." No matter, even average pizza was better than cooking for myself on a Sunday afternoon.

    I thought about what wine to bring on Christmas Eve, which was more pleasant than watching our Washington football team's standard poor performance. The Ravens on the other channel weren't having much better luck. I reviewed the bottles I had set aside at home versus what Judy might cook. For some reason, I was reluctant to just ask her what we would be eating. Maybe I would stop at my favorite liquor store tomorrow for some ideas.

    The next day after some good progress on *Waverly,* and a little work on the drone opinion, I did just that and came away with a couple of bottles of a nice California Meritage to pair with a chardonnay and riesling I had at home. I planned to bring all of them, since my juvenile nature still prevented me from asking Judy the simple question regarding her menu.

    I also made a stop at a nearby jewelry store and picked out a bracelet I thought she would like. We hadn't exchanged gifts at Christmas since our divorce, even when we celebrated the holiday together with the kids. For some reason, it seemed the thing to do this year.

    Tuesday was a short day at the court, the brethren gathering for a holiday lunch before heading off hither and yon for their various personal gatherings. I had told the clerks they could have the week off, but not surprisingly; all were working away. Even on Christmas Eve, three of the four of them were there in the morning, perhaps longer. I don't know; I left at noon. The Chief, Romo, Perry, and obviously Judy, were the others staying in town.

    Arriving at Judy's promptly at six, my arms laden with wine bottles, I entered to a cacophony of incredible smells, beef of some kind at the center. I set down the bottles and Judy looked over the labels, making pleasurable sounds at my choices. Based on what my nose told me, I opened the reds to let them breathe.

    Carrying the riesling, I followed Judy into the kitchen, and pulled the cork on the already chilled bottle, and poured each of us a glass. She opened the oven and pulled out a massive standing rib roast to rest before carving.

    "Who's coming to dinner? You, me, and the Third Infantry Regiment from Fort Myer?" I asked.

    "I couldn't find a smaller one in the store," she said. "You can have roast beef sandwiches for lunch for a few days instead of those disgusting peanut butter and jelly ones that you crush in that old briefcase."

    I just nodded. She was right about the PB&Js, but I loved that old briefcase.

Judy worked on the mashed potatoes and some sort of casserole side dish, while I sat, eyeing the roast and sipping riesling. She placed salad and rolls on the table.

"You can start slicing the roast now. It's rested long enough," she instructed.

It fell off the bone and sliced up into gorgeous juicy rare red slabs that I put on the platter she had ready. I left three quarters of it whole on the cutting board and there was still twice as much as we would consume on the platter.

I poured each of us a nice serving of the Meritage. I'm not a wine glass snob, but the stemware Judy had was magnificent and showed off the bouquet from the massive wine beautifully. The taste was even better. We clinked the glasses together.

"Merry Christmas," she said.

"The same to you," I responded.

For me, it doesn't get any better than meat, potatoes, and a great red wine. You can keep those big plates with a tiny presentation of something using unrecognizable ingredients built up in colorful layers four inches high that is the rage in fancy restaurants here in DC.

I had seconds of the beef, leaving much less on the platter than I thought would be there. Dessert was chocolate and spectacular.

We took the remaining half of the second bottle of red out to the couch, both of us weaving a little. I topped off each of our glasses, took a big sip from mine, and reached into the pocket of my sport coat for the box the girl at the jewelry store had wrapped so nicely for me.

"Merry Christmas," I said, handing it to Judy. Her eyes glowed, probably mostly from the wine, but there was a little surprise there too.

"Harry, you didn't need to…"

"Go ahead and open it," I said.

She ripped the paper off and opened the box, her eyes going wide.

"It's gorgeous," she said, raising the diamond and garnet bracelet into the light. The next thing I knew, she kissed me, hard, on the mouth. I was too surprised to say a word.

I awoke with a start, light streaming through the windows. I wasn't on the couch where I'd spent the last holiday night at Judy's. No, I was in a bed, and it wasn't mine. I had my boxers on, at least, and then I remembered. They had definitely been off earlier. Looking to my right, I saw Judy asleep, wearing my shirt. That was going to make a silent exit rather difficult. The other details of the night that I remembered I'll keep to myself in case future grandchildren read this. Yes, that is another hint to my son and daughter.

I got up, started the coffee, and we had a leisurely breakfast after Judy roused herself. I was more comfortable once I was able to get my shirt back. Our small talk was only slightly awkward, more on my end than hers. I admit to some internal discomfort, or maybe it was just the casserole side dish from last night disagreeing with my digestive system, but probably not.

Judy kissed me again at the door.

"Thanks for the present," she said as I left, leaving me wondering if she meant the bracelet or something else.

New Year's Eve was our next holiday together, but this time we were at Romo's house. Like me, she had bought a classic DC brownstone after her confirmation. Unlike mine, hers had a gourmet kitchen that any chef in the city would envy. Judy, Perry, and I all brought wine and champagne, leaving the cooking to Chef Romo.

Judy wore her new bracelet, and Romo and Perry spent a solid ten minutes examining it in detail, making almost cooing bird sounds while I sat observing. Perry got so close, for a minute I thought he was going to pull a jeweler's loupe out of his pocket. When he finally raised his head, he looked at me and winked. I felt blood rush to my cheeks, which intensified as I was embarrassed to be blushing like a teenager, which in turn sent more blood to my face turning it even redder, and so on.

We were told to come hungry. For myself, having eaten at Romo's before, I consumed nothing since half an English muffin and coffee at breakfast. Romo prepared a classic Italian meal with all the courses. An apertivo started us off. Champagne from Perry and some olives and cheeses, eaten gathered around the massive island in the kitchen while we watched the master cook.

An antipasta followed; a charcuterie type platter filled with salami, cheeses, and fresh breads. We sat down in the dining room for the primi course, an amazing pasta dish with truffles. I have no idea what it was called, just that it was delicious. I opened a couple bottles of the Oregon pinot noirs I brought while Romo carried out a platter with two roast ducks for the secondi with roasted potatoes as a side dish. We were a solid hour into the meal by this point.

After we all helped clear those dishes, an insalata course was served, followed by fruit and cheese, the formaggie frutta, she called it. Dolce or dessert was an entire separate table in the living room filled with a huge selection of Italian cookies, tiramisu, and espresso or coffee. Decaf coffee was my personal choice, but I was in the minority. A limoncello followed, the digestive, which got us ready to crack the Veuve Cliquot Brut brought by Judy for the midnight toast. I figured I would eat again on the third or fourth of January.

Conversation flowed easily throughout the night. Romo and I had socialized regularly for years, making a trio since Perry's appointment to the court. Judy fit in seamlessly, for which I was glad.

Perry was "balling in the conversation zone," as he described it. Sports was, as usual, a major focus of the repartee. Having won a Super Bowl ring with the New York Giants, Perry was dismissive, to be kind, of Romo's Jets, who had a chance at a wildcard berth this season. Of course, she was also a Yankees fan. My bottom-dwelling Cincinnati Reds and Chicago Bears got me sympathy from both, although each team was improving. Neither of them was old enough to remember the glory days of the Big Red Machine, but had seen my mid 80s Bears. Judy's Eagles fandom was resoundingly booed in a town where at least some allegiance to the disappointing Commanders was as much a requirement as a DC driver's license.

Not surprisingly, Judy had no problem holding her own with Perry. She hit him with a position-by-position destruction of the current Giants offense and defense. Perry looked at me during this exchange which I read as saying "you da man," having been married to Judy, but he also might have just been still hungry. Body language and looks are not my specialty.

Romo also gave him no mercy. "What's the matter, you pussy, can't handle a woman knowing football," she laughed.

Perry stuttered, an unusual reaction for the normally loquacious and articulate justice, upon receipt of the trash talk, at which he usually excelled. I laughed, eyeing the dessert table in the distance through the doorway to the living room. One must have their priorities straight.

Romo's place was a three bedroom. We had all arrived assuming we weren't driving home that night. Judy and Perry took the two spare rooms, and I had the quite comfortable living room couch.

That was a necessity since even though he was younger, Perry's six-and-a-half-foot frame was not built for couches. There were a couple sly comments about me sneaking into Judy's room, which I deliberately ignored. I wanted to believe the look on Judy's face implied she wasn't against it. But I was a good boy and remained comfortably settled on the couch until morning.

      We all rose within minutes of each other, took care of morning routines, and then worked our way through strong coffee and amazing pastries laid out by our host, forgetting about any promises not to eat again for multiple days. I made it home in plenty of time for a couple bowl games, amused by the odd naming rights. I thought the Home Depot Rigid Tools bowl coupled with a variety of erectile dysfunction commercials which aired during the game to be borderline prurient, but quite funny. I looked forward to going back to work the next morning, a strange feeling compared with how I'd started the term.

8

On the Monday of our first week back in session after the new year, Judy's first majority decision came down. Per tradition, it was unanimous, in this case an uninteresting Indian dispute, Native American, to be politically correct, argued early in her tenure. Even Firewater yawned through it. Oral had been so boring, not only did I not write about it here, but I completed two levels of my game in the allotted hour.

Judy near glowed as she read the synopsis of the result from the bench, rightfully so. One's first majority opinion was an important milestone. I still remember mine; *Snodgrass v IRS,* a tax case which has been cited a record zero times by lower courts or in the law reviews. Obviously not *Marbury v Madison* level of importance.[1]

After announcing the opinion, the only one released that day, we heard a single case, brought against the Audubon Society over the naming of some tiny bird brought by a professor of ornithology at a far-right conservative Christian college, alleging the name was a copyright infringement, as the Old Testament had used a portion of it describing something satanic. Or at least I think that's what it was about. All I knew is it made my head hurt, and the now normal questioning from Judy's end of the bench didn't help.

I did look up surreptitiously—I was more conscious of my body language while on the bench now—when Judy hit the professor's counsel with three phrases from the Old Testament that had been widely used in books, television, etc. to see if he thought all those were copyright violations as well. An unqualified yes got him a smile from

---

[1] The IRS won, as they usually do. Having spent the better part of my life writing briefs and decisions as a lawyer and judge, respectively, I'm now incapable of writing anything more complex than a Christmas card that doesn't have at least one footnote, so here it is.

Judy, which I had seen before. That was her "you dumbass" smile, which I had experienced multiple times while we were married. I wondered why we were wasting our time with this turd of a case, while my point total continued to increase. This was one I had no intention of writing one word on, unless I had totally misread the flow of the argument.

Back in chambers, Leslie and I went through the changes to *Waverly*. Her draft, and four or five rounds of my revisions, as well as the other clerks reading and commenting on it led up to this point. That was sufficient for a twelve-page opinion.

"Looks good, Leslie. Go ahead and send it to the printer for circulation to the other Justices; usual number of copies," I said. Since a leaked decision back in the Robert's court days, draft opinion distribution would occasionally be limited, but this was far from a case where that would be a concern.

"Great, I'll send it right away, sir," Leslie said.

The print shop was a vestige of the past, but something I still liked even with the availability of email and other electronic methods of distributing our work internally. Romo, Perry, and Jose, I think, typically read draft opinions on screens, but I preferred paper. I hadn't asked Judy her practice. The print shop would send both paper and electronic copies to the various chambers for the folks to do as they pleased. By the following morning, they had distributed it to the justices and clerks, not needing a lot of time for something that short.

I figured it would be a couple weeks before we saw Judy's dissent. And there might be a comment or two from one of the others in the majority, but those should be easily accommodated.

Boy, was I wrong.

Judy's dissent arrived around 4:30 PM as I was starting to pack it in for the day. I put it on the pile of things to be looked at, and folded up the brown bag my peanut butter and jelly sandwich and whatever forgettable snack I brought with me had been in, and slid it into my briefcase with the ever-present pack of seldom used sticky notes, and my cell phone. If it wasn't a day when I was going to hang around for a cocktail, I liked to head out around this time.

Putting on my overcoat, I walked into the outer room, said good evening to the clerks and Edith, and continued through the main door into the corridor. Turning to my right, I almost walked into Judy.

"I was just coming to see you. Did you get my dissent?" she asked.

"Indeed I did," I said, trying to sound cheerful while hoping this wouldn't take long. I'd found this to be kind of a sweet spot traffic wise in my commute. Ten minutes from now, my ride would be extended by at least a half hour.

"What did you think?" she continued.

"I have no idea. I haven't looked at it." I did look at my watch. It was going to be close.

"Why?"

"Because it just came, and I'm going home," I said. I tried not to sound patronizing, but didn't think it worked.

"Do you have it with you? I'd be happy to go over it together," she said.

"It's on the pile for tomorrow. I'm not taking any work home tonight," I said, now resigned to an extended ordeal in traffic.

She crossed her arms, like she used to when lecturing one of the kids about cleaning up their room when they were small. Don't roll your eyes, whatever you do, I told myself.

"I don't understand how you can be blasé when I worked so hard to get this to you so promptly."

"Because I don't want to, don't have to, and am not going to read it tonight. I don't work for you, Judy. I didn't ask for your dissent immediately. To be honest, I don't give a shit if the case comes down two days, two weeks, or two months from now."

"But…"

"No buts," I said, gently motioning her around the corner to avoid the ears on the traffic that was beginning to increase in the hallway, as others left to go home.

"Yes but. You were the one in here working the day after Thanksgiving. I thought there was an expectation…"

Now I understood. I laughed quietly.

"No, Judy, I was in here because I have no life, couldn't think of anything else to do, and it was quiet. You, me, all of us, there's no judgment or expectation that you have to work eighty hours a week. Sure, you're going to put in a bunch of extra hours the first few years. I did, we all did, and I'm sure you remember it from when we were married. I guess I didn't explain it well enough when we talked that day."

She looked a little bit relieved, but still conflicted.

"Screw this, go get your coat and let's go to that pizza place again," I said. She brightened at the idea.

We sat at the same table as the last time. More aware, we ordered a regular sized pie, not the eighteen-inch monstrosity we tried to consume previously. A bottle of another good, but not expensive Chianti was my choice. Even the same waiter, who seemed to recognize us, as past customers luckily, not justices.

As we waited for our pizza, Judy scrolled through some news on her phone, and reading upside down, I saw there was one of the myriad pieces on the royal family. It gave me a thought as I looked over a bit closer to see what she was reading.

"Look at that princess in England. She can't leave her house—okay—castle, but you know what I mean, without somebody writing about what she's wearing, who designed the dress, 'cause she can almost never wear pants except if she's going someplace where that dress might blow up, ala Marilyn Monroe, which I wouldn't complain about, though…"

"Pig," Judy said.

"Guilty as charged, but here's the thing. Among these writers, there's literally people who get paid to know she wore that particular dress one time two years ago on March 12th when she took her kids to school."

"Where do you get this shit, Harry?" She asked with a crooked grin, trying not to laugh, I was sure.

"Oh, you know me. I sit around all the time thinking these big thoughts," I said. That got the laugh I was hoping for.

The pizza arrived. It was as good as the last time. The place was busy, doing a good business for this early. In DC, dining before six constitutes early, and even that's questionable. None of the "society" people or politicians show their faces in restaurants before seven. The chief justice, of course, was among those who wouldn't be caught dead dining prior to that hour.

After slice number two, Judy brought the conversation back to work, as I knew she would.

"I think you'll find my dissent interesting," she started.

"I'm sure I will. Most dissents are interesting. In some ways, writing dissents is far more fun than a majority."

"How so?"

"A dissent can be a little looser in form. You're writing for a future court you hope will come your direction or to get the attention of Congress. And before you ask, don't assume you're going to persuade anyone to flip their vote. I told you, a dissent changes my vote, most of our votes, maybe once every couple years, at best."

She got quiet for a minute. "Seems like a lot of work for little result."

"I don't think so. It provides the judges, lawyers, and more importantly legislators and the public, if they bother to read it, more context about a case. Dissents prompt changes in statutes if Congress thinks the majority got it wrong or if they disagree with the outcome, and those are two different things, which I don't need to tell you. At least a couple times a term, I vote for a decision I think sucks because that's the way the law is written." Judy raised her eyebrows at that, but said nothing, busy chewing.

"Over time, a dissent can become a majority as the court membership changes. On a less professional level, sometimes it just feels damn good to take a poke at the majority," I smiled. "And back to the other topic from earlier, it's entirely up to you if you want to be a workaholic justice. We have some, Romo for one, and I've served with a couple others. All the clerks work a brutal schedule, but hey, it's only for a year, and when they're done, most of them can easily get jobs starting at more than we make. Not a bad deal."

I'd hoped we'd finished off the work discussion for the night. Her next comment would tell me if I was successful or not.

"I think I've got room for cannolis tonight," she said.

The next morning, I pulled her dissent from my inbox and smiled. My opinion was twelve pages; her dissent thirty. It was, to no surprise, well written and reasoned. It was also still going to lose. From skimming it, I thought I might end up adding a footnote or two to the majority, but nothing more.

Edith brought in the morning coffee, and the clerks filed in.

"Did you get a chance to look at the *Waverly* dissent, sir?" Leslie asked.

"I took a quick look. I'll read it in more detail later, but I'm not seeing anything requiring any major changes in our draft. Maybe add a footnote or two to answer the most significant arguments. Don't get carried away."

"Yes sir," she said, looking a bit disappointed that I wasn't going to turn her loose to tear apart the dissent in our opinion.

I grabbed the box on my desk, opened it, and told the clerks to enjoy some cannolis. I'd picked up extras last night. The luscious filling was a marvelous addition to our morning coffee, and everyone went back to work in a better mood.[2]

The case we were hearing today was another doozy. Four hours of argument again so multiple attorneys general could each get their ten minutes so they could report to the citizens of their respective states how they had stood up for them in front of the Supreme Court.

This one was about chickens. The agriculture department and associated federal food regulatory agencies had promulgated revised regulations after years of hearings, debate, comments, and meetings on how many minutes outside and how many square inches a chicken had to have to be labeled "free range" once it had been chopped, plucked, and packaged for the supermarket. The states were arguing the federal regulations were too restrictive, hurt their producers economically, and the department had not followed the proper procedures before issuing the rules which they said required even more hearings, debate and meetings than had already been held. California, of course, took a third view that the agriculture regulators should require even more space per bird, and a certain minimum number of hours of sunlight to cluck around in. I was surprised they didn't ask for a masseuse for the chickens.

None of the parties, the states, or the agriculture department, gave a damn what the chickens might think; whether they liked living in a cage they could barely turn around in until they became ingredients for Colonel Sanders. Since I never read the label on the rare occasion I visited the poultry section of the supermarket, neither did I. No matter the label, it all tasted like, wait for it, chicken.

Chef Romo asked more questions than Judy. Since she sat right next to me, it distracted me from my game, although the sarcastic comments she whispered throughout the marathon were amusing. By

---

[2] While I worked hard to avoid any reference in the text to "leave the gun, take the cannoli's" I find it impossible to leave out completely, so here it is, Puzo, Mario, The Godfather, New York, G.P. Putnam's Sons, 1969.

the time the chief finally uttered the long waited for words "the case is submitted," my rear teeth were floating, and based on the company I had at the urinals in the restroom off our gowning area, I wasn't the only one.

On Friday, the chief's lecture on the chicken case, as we'd taken to calling it, was a first-year law student review of *Chevron*. The bottom line of this almost universally disliked precedent, is courts were to defer to the interpretation of the agency involved when Congress was not specific in drafting a statute, which they never were. When it got to me, I limited my comments to one word.

"Affirm," I said, which in this case meant I sided with the Agriculture Department or the chickens, depending on your perspective. The chief, for reasons known only to him, but which we'd read about in his dissent, had gone the other way, which left Olive Oyl as senior, and she gave the opinion to Romo.

We then moved on to some cert petitions. *Brown v IRS* (or the vibrator case as I referred to it, though not in mixed company), was first up, and as I predicted, Perry voted to take it after his comments on various sex toys and their uses that turned Olive Oyl's face the color of a strawberry. To my surprise, there was a second vote to hear it. When Judy voted to grant, it was 7-2, well short of the needed four, but made it a sure thing that Perry would ask to have it put over for discussion again next week, which he immediately did.

Following conference, Judy, Romo, Perry, and I adjourned to my chambers for cocktails. The bourbon, vodka, and scotch flowed freely, over ice and neat. A snowstorm was predicted overnight, a crippling four inches forecasted. The District, and Maryland and Virginia suburbs would shut down for two inches. With four, the milk and bread shelves of grocery stores would look like a war zone, the beer aisle decimated, and the city would be lucky to reopen on Monday. For as long as I'd lived here, I still hadn't gotten used to the panic produced by snow flurries in the forecast. It didn't have to snow, just be predicted.

"By the way, I'm having a Super Bowl party at my place, and you're all invited." I changed the subject from the half assed blizzard. The game was in a couple weeks.

"You're cooking?" Romo gave me the evil eye.

"If you call expertly wielding take-out and delivery menus like the master I am cooking, then yes." She laughed. I knew she would bring something no matter what I said that would outclass the pizza and wings I planned by orders of magnitude.

We finished our drink, and everyone got ready to leave, sliding into the middle of Friday rush hour. I threw my overcoat over my arm, grabbed my briefcase, and started for the door, bringing up the rear. Judy slowed, letting Romo and Perry exit, and turned back toward me.

"How about I pick up some food and come over to your place? We can watch the snow start," she said.

"You're not worried about the roads?"

"Me? Four inches, not hardly."

"Sure, why not," I agreed. I had no idea what was in my refrigerator or cupboards if I were to make something, so it worked out nicely.

"Okay, see you in an hour or so," she said.

Around 7:00 PM, my bell rang, and I opened the front door to find Judy, her arms overloaded with bags, a large tote with a long strap over her shoulder. She handed me a couple of the bags, dropped the tote by the door, and followed me into the kitchen. We set the bags on the counter and she shrugged out of her coat, draping it over the chair. She was dressed for comfort in jeans and a big sweater, probably remembering I never kept the heat on too high.

"What's all this?" I said, looking at numerous bags of various sizes inside other bags.

"Food," she said.

"This I know. Something smells great. I thought you were bringing dinner for you and me. I wasn't expecting the NY Giants offensive line too."

"Don't worry about it. Get out a couple of plates, preferably not paper, and open something for us to drink," she ordered.

Judy started pulling Chinese food containers from one of the larger bags. Not my favorite but she had picked out plenty of things I did like. I figured a couple of Heinekens, the beer that happened to be in the refrigerator, was the easiest thing as I had no idea what kind of wine went with Chinese. I opened both bottles and slid one over to her and she took a swig.

"What are you watching?" she asked, seeing the glow of the television through the doorway.

"The Wizards are playing. Losing, more accurately, but it's better than the news or game shows."

"True," she said, stuffing an eggroll in her mouth. "Let's go watch." She picked up her plate and beer. I grabbed mine and a couple more beers. Settling in on my couch, we ate, drank, and watched the Wizards perform as predicted, losing 104 to 82. The next thing I knew, I woke up, still on the couch. The news was on, the weather guy droning on about the snow that had already started, from what I could see out the window. Glancing around, I noted the dishes were gone and so was Judy's bag by the door. I wasn't the only one who had mastered the quiet get-away, I figured.

Turning the television off, I headed up to bed. Teeth brushed, I kicked off my shoes, dropped my pants on the floor in the dark bedroom, and slid into bed. Immediately I recognized something different when Judy threw her arm across me and her hair tickled my neck.

"What the…"

"Shhh, go to sleep. I'm tired," she yawned.

So, I did.

We awoke in the morning within seconds of each other.

"I'll start some coffee," I said, pulling some sweatpants on, and starting down the stairs. She came down a few minutes later, wearing my robe. I poured us each a cup, and she kissed me on the cheek. We sat, sipped, and looked at the snow, still coming down. It looked like the weather guessers had gotten it wrong. There wasn't four inches outside; it appeared more like fourteen, and it was still coming down.

Judy went into one of the bags on the counter, and pulled out a package of English muffins. The big shoulder bag, English muffins; I'm a bit slow, but it was becoming clearer to me that this overnight was planned.

"See, I remembered," she laughed.

Another cup of coffee and the English muffins were toasted. We ate, drank, and watched the snow some more. Finished with breakfast, I looked around.

"So, what do you want to do now?" I asked.

Judy put down her cup, smiled, took my hand, and led me to the stairs.

By the time we came back downstairs, it was dark again. For those of you thinking salacious thoughts, I will tell you the majority of the time, but admittedly not all, was spent…sleeping. Judy dug through her magic food bags and out came additional supplies which she combined with odds and ends I had laying around the kitchen, to turn into a delicious dinner.

After we ate, I made us each a drink and we took them back upstairs to bed. Settling in under the covers with the television we watched news coverage of the snowstorm, channel surfing all the DC networks. Fire trucks with chains were crawling to calls. Plows were working to open major arteries; Metro busses and trains were shut down. The National Guard was on call. The news reporters milked the white stuff for everything it was worth, predicting it could be well into next week before conditions improved.

Finishing my drink and with the droning of the interchangeable news people continuing, I fell back to sleep. Judy watched a west coast college basketball game, she later told me, before also resuming her slumber.

On Sunday morning, the snow having stopped sometime while we slept, and after more English Muffins and coffee, I went out to help Judy dig out her car. Then I slowly dug out my own, trying to avoid the need for the currently overworked paramedics due me having a heart attack, while she made the short drive home.

Basketball and left-over Chinese food filled the rest of my day, and Monday morning, I arrived at the court bright and early, exceptionally well rested after the amount of sleep I got over the snowy weekend. Our cases that day had been switched to virtual, an easy process as the court had plenty of experience with it during Covid and the technology now was even better. Most of the justices, including Judy, stayed home. The chief, Romo, and I all participated from our respective chambers. Luckily the two arguments were yawners, and I was able to knock off two levels of my current game without working very hard.

On Tuesday, the chief pushed the single argument we had scheduled to the afternoon, as Firewater was having difficulty due to the roads out in Damascus in Montgomery County, but he made it in by lunchtime. In the city, some side streets still hadn't seen a plow, garbage was piling up with postponed collections, and the mayor was being blamed for every fender bender, slip, trip, and fall in the entire city. All-in-all, a typical Washington snow storm.

By Thursday, it was sixty-five degrees and complaints had turned to the heat and street flooding due to blocked storm drains. I started planning for the Super Bowl party. It wasn't like organizing the

Normandy invasion, but getting takeout and delivery orders in early was critical for a successful party on that particular day in this town. Probably everywhere else too. Our new favorite pizza place supplanted my previous supplier.

My clerks were invited. Each justice handled social events with their clerks differently. Some hosted monthly dinners or lunches. I tried to keep things more casual, and less demanding for myself and the clerks. My annual Super Bowl party, a nice dinner out at a restaurant in the first couple months, and a term-ending barbeque, were standard for me. The Super Bowl party was also a chance for the clerks to interact with a few other justices with their hair down, so to speak.

The party was great. The game, not so much. The teams were not of any real interest to me, or anyone else in the group, apart from Perry. Houston beat the Arizona Cardinals 38-14. The first quarter looked like a pre-season game until both teams got their nerves settled. The best part of the game was being able to mute the sound and take advantage of our personal play-by-play and color commentary courtesy of Perry.

He'd spent the previous week doing film study on both teams and knew their tendencies cold. He could, and did, tell us what play the offense and defense were going to run before the teams lined up, in most cases. And since he was not on broadcast television, he could do it in his own inimitable style, which included colorful profanity on numerous occasions.

It was a good thing those on both teams who played linebacker, Perry's former position, couldn't hear his running critique of their performance. The clerks were enthralled, as was Judy. Romo and I had seen this performance before and got more of a kick out of seeing the reaction of the others to it. The clerks were also not used to hearing one justice refer to another justice as "baby," and no, it did not come from me.

No wallflower, Judy enjoyed pushing Perry's buttons, and had come prepared, having memorized his Superbowl performance statistics.

A missed tackle on a punt return early in the game got it started. Perry pounced all over the poor special teams player. Judy pounced on Perry.

"You missed exactly the same tackle on a kickoff return in the third quarter of your game," Judy said, and reached over to clink her beer bottle with Romo.

"Judy, baby, it wasn't close to the same play, and the fucking zebra missed the hold on me," he countered, knowing exactly the play she referred to.

"Bullshit, have another piece of pizza," Judy said, smiling. Perry had already moved on to commenting about the clock management of the Texans.

The opinion Judy and I shared about the pizza was ratified by the group.

"How come I didn't know about this freaking place? This is as good as the best I've had in Brooklyn," Romo gave her ringing endorsement, working on her third piece, still in the first quarter, diet be damned.

The clerks, and Perry, as expected, attacked it like lions after gazelles. The five pizzas I picked up just before the game started were gone halfway through the second quarter. Luckily, I had another four coming at halftime, along with a gross of chicken wings from another place. It was like having teenagers in the house again.

The second half ravenous consumption of food continued with the arrival of the pizza and wings; all hot of course, no mild wings in my house. Romo laid out a spread of fresh bread, salami, cheese, and olives that rivaled what one could get at a five-star restaurant. Perry brought six cases of beer with him, from Budweiser to Dos Equis, understanding the clerks were not that long out of college, and probably not interested in the Chiantis I'd opened. Judy, having raised two children to adulthood, baked multiple trays of brownies, understanding what the youngsters, and me of course, would enjoy.

The banter from the clerks was enjoyable. Leslie and John debated the quality of the quarterback play. She did blush a bit after noting that the Houston quarterback was cute when Perry loudly agreed with her. "Sweet ass," was Perry's comment.

With Houston up 38-7 with eight minutes to go in the fourth quarter, it was obvious the game was over. Houston started using their depth chart starting with about four minutes remaining. The brownies were getting far more attention than the third-string quarterback, even though he was cute too. Arizona added seven in the last minute, but it meant nothing. Perry, though, was still laser focused on the game until the last second ticked off the clock.

The clerks had drunk enough beer that they could relax with justices not their own. Super Bowl Sunday was one of the few days each year Perry wore his ring. They went from sideways glances in the first quarter to asking if they could try it on by the fourth. Perry was happy to oblige, I was sure pictures of the ring on various much smaller fingers, would be scattered across social media accounts, text messages, and other apps these youngsters used that I've never heard of.

Our next set of oral arguments started on Tuesday after the Super Bowl. The football fans amongst the brethren, pretty much all of us except the chief, had prevailed upon him to leave the Monday after game day open. It gave counsel and any parties a day for travel, preparation, and what have you instead of losing Superbowl Sunday to one or more of those.

That said, the first case up deserved no sympathy, at least for one side. It was a real head shaker for me. The junior senator from California was making a good living, not from his substantial government salary, but moonlighting as a television huckster selling cheap knives, herbal pills which would purportedly cure the flu, prevent warts, and grow hair, and supposedly had a variety of other benefits. He did not say where the hair would grow. He would get in front of a television camera and sell pretty much any product somebody, any somebody, would pay him to endorse.

Some folks found that the knives wouldn't slice butter, hot or not, and fell apart the first time in the dishwasher. A group that took the pills soon had warts and hair in unpleasant places, filed suit against the honorable gentleman, as only ninety-nine people in the country were required to call him. The Senate has some strange traditions.

The senator, in his defense, claimed that the speech or debate clause of the constitution protected him, and allowed him to say pretty much whatever he wanted to. The district court judge, having half a brain, rejected this categorically. However, when he appealed to the ninth circuit, the three-judge panel he drew was a group that had apparently been underqualified to be school crossing guards so they somehow became appeals court judges. From the reasoning in their unanimous opinion, one wonders how they got their robes on before court.

The full circuit denied the plaintiff request for an *en banc* hearing, a fancy lawyer word for rehearing the case before all the judges. They were either as ill-qualified as the original panel, or wanted to watch us slap the shit out of the first three.

When we discussed the cert petition in conference, I wanted to reverse without any hearing, and send it back to the circuit directing them to look at the district court decision with a two-word order, "try again." The others voted to grant, feeling my approach a bit harsh, and that a sitting senator deserved the courtesy of a being heard. The only good news was that it appeared that none of the brethren agreed with the senator's contention.

The Founders wanted open debate among our representatives. They didn't want them punished for their opinions. If Senator Moron wanted to get up in front of the chamber and say Bill XYZ would result in the US puppy population perishing when all it really does was revise the tax code, that was protected speech, and the only way he could be punished, as it were, was at the ballot box.

Article I, Section 6, Clause 1 stated in part "…and for any Speech or Debate in either House, they shall not be questioned in any other place." While our decisions had not read it restrictively (funny how the originalists had no problem with those precedents) to cover campaign speech, and so on, there was a line. Some senators and representatives thought that anything that came out of their mouth during working hours was covered by the clause. A minority even thought anything they mumbled in their sleep should be included.[3]

"How about you contribute a million dollars to my reelection campaign, Mr. Lobbyist, and I'll vote for that bill you want," said Senator Moron.

"Isn't that bribery?" asked Mr. Lobbyist. Not really, any lobbyist that I've ever met would just smile and open their check book.

"No, I'm covered under the speech or debate clause," said Senator Moron.

---

[3] If this were an opinion, I could and would cite a dozen cases here supporting my interpretation, but will restrain myself, except for adding this third footnote. Sorry.

That's essentially the argument the senator from California was making with just a different set of facts.

So, on that Tuesday morning after the Super Bowl, the chief called the court to order and announced the case. The senator sat in the front row with his wife, smiling with a mouth full of capped and whitened teeth that sparkled.

His counsel opened with the traditional "thank you, Mr. Chief Justice, and may it please the court…" Before he got the first word of his argument out, Romo pounced.

"It's my impression that selling cheap, excuse me low-cost knives, has no connection to the senator's legislative responsibilities. Perhaps you can explain why I'm wrong."

The lawyer smiled; teeth almost as bright as the senator's, beneath his deceitful little mustache. He reminded me of the stereotypical used car salesman before he even started.

"Certainly, Justice Romaldini, the senator is communicating with his constituents, and the citizens at large, when he is describing the capabilities of the high-quality cutlery he so ardently believes in. Such communication is inherently controlled by the speech or debate clause."

"Try again, Mr. Snoffton. If you can't do better than that, we're all in for a long morning." I was as surprised as everyone else to hear my own voice.

"Um, I'm not sure how to respond, Justice Cashman."

"I think what Justice Cashman is saying, is that he does not find your argument remotely persuasive, and I will add, neither do I, and is hoping you can assist us in comprehending it," Romo said. The lawyer started stuttering.

Then came our master of the hypotheticals. "Let's say the senator asked twenty people to each give him five million dollars for which he would send them to Uranus on a rocket. If, as I assume we can agree, such a trip is fundamentally impossible, the funds received would be ill-gotten gains, and the senator liable for the falsities. Do you agree," Olive Oyl's chalkboard scratching voice sounded kind, but I knew this was like setting the cheese in a trap for the mouse.

"Thank you for the question, Madam Justice." The lawyer was already wiping his brow with a handkerchief.

"Space travel is a complex topic which the senator has great interest in. Conversations regarding it would fall under his responsibilities and hence be covered by the speech or debate clause and…"

"How about you answer the question that was asked?" He was in real trouble now. Judy was leaning forward, and not using her judge voice. This was her pissed-off wife tone, and it made the hair stand up on the back of my neck. "Is fraud is covered by the speech or debate clause or not. A simple yes or no will do," she glared at the simpleton.

I glanced at the senator. His smile was gone. There were worry lines crossing his forehead and a line of perspiration above his upper lip. His wife pretended she didn't know him.

"Uh, I'm not sure I agree that fraud…"

"So, the answer is yes," Judy shot back. This guy was up to his neck in quicksand.

I didn't think it possible, but it went downhill from there. Curious, I called one of the pages over and whispered a question, and they came back with a sheet of paper that gave this guy's background. Reading between the lines, he was one step up from an ambulance chaser. An ambulance chaser may have been a better choice as an advocate than the lawyer the senator chose. I had no idea how he'd gotten hooked up with the senator. I guess conmen attract other conmen.

By the time the clock mercifully wound down, he had been pummeled by all nine of us. Even the chief, who was usually the most deferential to advocates, got in a shot or two.

"Thank you, Mister Snoffton, your time has expired," the chief said, ending the Senator's time was the nicest thing anyone had said to the lawyer in thirty minutes.

Counsel for the folks who ended up with warts and hair in unwanted places, an experienced lawyer who had appeared before us several times, looked like he had swallowed a puppy, a broad smile on his face as he rose to the lectern. He spoke uninterrupted for ten minutes, damn near a modern record. Romo finally asked a technical question about one of the precedents he was discussing, more to give him a breather, I think, than to elicit any information. He went another five minutes or so and ran out of material. Advocates today expect to argue for fifteen minutes, tops, and spend most of their time answering questions.

"At this time, I have nothing further, unless there are additional questions, Mr. Chief Justice," he said, looking sheepish that he hadn't filled the entire half hour. That told me he was a smart guy, not trying to filibuster when he knew he'd checked all the boxes he needed to. The chief looked up and down the bench, and no one said a word.

"Thank you, Mr. Johnston. The case is submitted."

News outlets of every type destroyed the senator over the next two days. There were calls for his resignation from pundits on both sides of the conservative/liberal divide, and very uncomfortable comments from his fellow senators. He didn't resign, but did announce he had changed his mind about running for reelection, opening the floodgates to candidates for the primary in six months.

He also signed a deal to promote space trips, not to Uranus or any other planet, but to low earth orbit, which had been shown to be possible. I thought Olive Oyl should sue him for a finder's fee.

9

At conference on Friday, the discussion on the conman case, as I'd taken to calling it in chambers, went faster than normal. The chief, in an unusual turn of events, couldn't find enough material to fill his normal forty-five minutes. After thirty, during which he repeated himself a half dozen times, he concluded. The rest of us took a combined twenty to state our views.

Unanimous against the senator, as expected, the chief assigned the opinion to Perry, who looked like a kid at Christmas. Before we moved on, I gestured to get Perry's attention.

"I'm joining whatever you write, but I'm telling you in advance I will be writing a concurrence, brother."

Perry winked and blew me a kiss. I shook my head, and the others laughed. They all knew how pissed off I was about this case.

We had a few cert petitions to review. I'm not sure how they made it this far, but somebody had thought they were worth our time to discuss, however briefly.

The first one was *Trump v. The Witch Who Used to be NYS Attorney General.* Along with it was the counter suit, *Letita James v. The Orange Haired Orangutang Who Used to be President.* The two had reached a point in their decade-long legal battles that they could no longer say each other's names, and for some reason, the lower courts were allowing it. Since at the circuit court level they upheld the district court's dismissal of both suits, this was an easy one. We weren't touching either or both with a ten-foot pole. We denied cert with no comments.

The next one was easy as well. Timex was being sued over a watch model that lost a minute a week from the set time. The warranty was quite clear that time accuracy was not covered. Not exactly surprising for a twenty-three-dollar watch. The suit wanted class action status, which would have required Timex to pay a lot of money or replace a lot of watches, which wouldn't have worked any better than the original ones, assuming they lost.

The district court denied class action status but let the claim on the single watch stand. Timex offered the plaintiff a two hundred dollar watch to settle the case. Apparently out of principle, or spite, the rocket scientist declined and appealed to the circuit court, which in their opinion said "seriously?" Yes, I'm paraphrasing. The watch owner then came to us. We let the circuit court decision stand with no comment. And people wonder why the court system is so busy.

I walked back to my chambers with Perry. Jubilant is the mildest description of his reaction to the conman case assignment. He strutted down the marble corridor on his long legs. I was almost jogging to keep up with him.

"This is the best fucking opinion I've had all term," he said.

"Dude, it was unanimous," I said, huffing a bit with the exertion of keeping up to him. I only talked like that when he reverted to his football personae. The two of us walked through my outer office, and I pointed to John to follow us into my chambers. I almost laughed out loud at the confused look on his face as he rose and came along.

I dropped my leather portfolio on the table and opened my globe, taking out two glasses, and then feeling like a poor host, a third. I dropped ice cubes into mine and Perry's, added bourbon to both, and then looked at John.

"You want one?"

"Uh, certainly, Justice Cashman," he said even more confused now.

I decided not to ask, and added ice to the third glass, poured two fingers of bourbon, but surreptitiously added a little water for him. I felt like a new dad watering down my kid's apple juice.

I handed out the drinks, and the three of us settled in around my table. Perry raised his glass in a toast.

"You're going to get to work on the best opinion of the fucking term," he said, looking at John. I looked at John, shook my head almost imperceptibly.

"Don't get too excited," I said.

"Hell yes, get excited," Perry said, his body language, although seated looked like he'd just scored a touchdown.

"The court is unanimous in holding against the conman, I mean senator, and Justice Jacobs has been assigned the opinion," I said in an even tone, trying to bring things back to earth. The confused visage remained as John nervously consumed half his drink. He coughed, trying to muffle the noise, not used to near full-strength liquor.

"I'm going to concur, as I have some things I want to say on the case, and this one is yours. But contrary to the impression Justice Jacobs may be giving, we're not doing extensive work on this. A couple pages at most." Now he understood, and the pressure drained from his body.

"Pull together what you have and we'll sit down Monday and I'll give you my thoughts. You can work with that for now, but then we'll wait until we get Perry's, uh, Justice Jacob's draft before we finalize things."

"Yes sir," he said, finishing his drink and standing. "Will there be anything else?"

"Nope, have a good weekend," I said, and he almost wobbled, heading for the door. I'd have to add a bit more water the next time.

A few minutes after John left, my door opened, and Judy and Romo strolled in. I could tell from the look on their faces they had been plotting something. Perry was too busy basking in his joy over getting the opinion to notice, much less understand, that whatever this was would impact him as well. I'd make sure of it.

I rose to go to the globe bar and be a good host, but the two of them waved me off and walked over to fix their own drinks. Once in hand, they came over and took the recently vacated chair and another. I looked at both, shaking my head.

"What's going on and what's it going to cost me?"

Romo looked stunned. She turned to Judy.

"How did you know? How did he know?"

"We were married and we were married," she said, the same answer to the two questions.

"Now that we have that out of the way, why don't you let me in on what's going on?"

Perry observed the conversation with a discernable level of disinterest, still not perceiving that this involved him as well. It was Romo who answered. I didn't know if this was part of the plan or spontaneous.

"We're all going for pizza tonight. The place you got it from for the Super Bowl Party," she said.

Now Perry perked up.

"How do you know I don't have a date tonight?" He asked.

"Because I didn't hear about any tight ass, pants filling stud at conference this afternoon," she fired right back at him. Both my drink and Judy's came out our noses.

"True," he said, looking sheepish. Then his face changed to a devilish grin. "That guy is tomorrow night, and he is hot and hung." Not having a mirror, I'm not sure if my face was redder or Judy's. I'd bet on mine.

"Right, good to know," Romo said, disbelief evident in her tone, while draining her glass. "We having one for the road or just going now?" It was obvious to me this outing was not optional.

Ever the practical one, Judy looked over at me. "Do you think we should get reservations?" I thought about it for a minute. Friday night, pizza, DC; probably a good idea. I reached back to my desk for the intercom to Edith, and pushed the button.

"Yes, Justice Cashman," came the immediate response.

"Edith, can you get me reservations for four at Luigi's in northwest for 6:30?" I asked.

"Certainly sir," she answered.

If it seems like we spend a lot of time eating out, talking about eating out, and food in general, you would be correct. Everyone in almost any governmental position in DC does. Arguably, a bit more government business gets done in restaurants and bars than on golf courses, although that's only because we have winter. I don't golf, in any event. I should, however, provide a disclaimer: judges don't do business outside their courtroom or chambers. We just like to eat.

The intercom buzzed, and Edith's voice announced, "you have reservations at 6:30 PM at Luigi's[4] under your name, sir." It was then I, figuratively, slapped my head. The anonymity Judy and I had so enjoyed there may have just been lost.

We had another round, then left for the restaurant. On arrival, I knew my fear was correct. Our previous waiter greeted us at the door,

---

[4] Not the real name, to protect our ability to get a table if this becomes a best seller. Wishful thinking. Yes, I know this is the fourth footnote.

recognized Judy and I, but when I said the name of the reservation, the color drained out of his face.

"Welcome back, Mr. Justice, sir. I have your table all ready for you," His eyes were big. Not what I wanted to see. I put my arm around his shoulders. It was time to channel my inner Pennsylvania politician, as it were.

"Please forget about any title my secretary used when she made this reservation. We just love the food here, and your service, and don't want anything different than how you treated us before." I reached my other hand out to shake his.

"My name's Harry," I said. He still looked uncomfortable, but a little less so.

"I'm Dominic, sir, uh, Harry," he said.

"Dominic," I half whispered in his ear, "just so you don't waste too much time looking things up back in the kitchen, this is the other Justice Cashman, Justice Jacobs, and Justice Romaldini. For your purposes, it's Harry, Judy, Perry, and Toni. And we really like pizza, beer, and wine. Especially yours. We okay?"

"Yes sir, I mean, Harry," he said, as we arrived at the table. He pulled out the chairs for Judy and Romo, and sweat beading on his forehead, left to grab the menus. When he returned, it looked like he'd relaxed a little bit.

"Dude, don't you get congressmen and senators in here?" Perry was sincerely interested, maybe a little confused by the reaction, as most restaurants he went to were used to government diners, but I wished he hadn't asked the question.

"Occasionally, sir, but we've never had the Supreme Court in here," he said, unable to keep the awe out of his voice. Perry laughed.

"Dude, there's 535 of them, just nine of us. It's cool. I'll tell you a secret; we're much nicer. What kind of beer you got on tap?"

Dominic smiled and relaxed and recited the beer menu, which he knew by heart.

A half hour later, we were deep into multiple pizzas and a couple bottles of Chianti. The pitcher of beer we had started with had been emptied before the first pie arrived.

"Damn, Harry, this is great," Perry said, letting out a soft belch. Judy gave him a look.

"Excuse me, Mom," he said. She looked around, made sure no one was watching, and shot him the finger. I almost choked on the pizza I was chewing. Perry just laughed and burped again, louder this time.

When we had consumed more pizza than any eight people should, the three of them ordered espresso. I was happy with a plain decaf coffee. Of course, we had to get the cannoli too.

"What gave you two this idea?" Perry asked what I'd been wondering.

"Just seemed like a good idea," Judy said.

"We'd been talking about the pizza on and off all week. It really takes me back to Brooklyn," Romo added.

The next morning, my phone rang. I looked down and saw it was Judy.

"What are you doing?" she asked without even a hello.

"Reading the paper, drinking coffee. It's Saturday. Why?" Another sign that I'm old fashioned, or just old, is how much I enjoy opening my front door in the morning and picking up a real newspaper, awaiting me on my porch.

"Meet me at Rock Creek Park."

Why?" Was she planning to have me killed, dispose of the body in the woods? What possible reason could there be for an unplanned meeting in the park?

"It's nice out. Let's go for a walk."

"It's fifty-five degrees. How is that nice?"

"Did your blood get thinned out living here? Pennsylvania Harry wouldn't think fifty-five was cold."

"Okay, I'm on my way."

I pulled in next to her a half hour later, and got out of my car, insulated coffee mug in hand.

"What took you so long?" she asked.

"I had to find heavy socks, get my coffee ready, find a hat…"

"You wuss, it's a beautiful sunny day."

"Whatever you say. Why did you want to come here?" I asked.

"Just exploring."

"Exploring? You used to live here."

"I lived here for two years when you came on the court before we divorced. You were never home—learning the job, I have a way better appreciation for that now—and the kids were young. I didn't go anywhere except work, home, and to their school stuff."

"Touche. I was a shithead back then. Confirmation then my first years on the court. My priorities were all messed up."

"You're right, but that's water under the bridge now. Isn't this place lovely?" She said, looking around, excited.

I turned, glanced here and there, trying to open myself to what she saw. It was nice, I had to admit. Still gray and mostly dormant, but the snow was gone. We started walking, strolling really. There were other people around doing the same thing but the park was far from crowded. I had my hands in my pockets to keep warm, but she was right, it was nice out.

Judy slipped her arm through mine as we walked. "I need to get a bike. This is a great place to ride," she said. I didn't respond and she changed the subject.

"Courtney called me." Our daughter. "We're invited to her house for Easter."

"She didn't call me," I said, slightly miffed at the exclusion.

"I told her I'd tell you." I would have liked to hear from her myself, but it wasn't worth getting excited about. Judy laughed, able to read my reaction.

"She does know we work together, see each other in the hallway, and so on."

"I told her I'd come and I would pass on the invitation to you. I'm not going to speak for you."

"No, no, I want to go."

"Great, you can drive. I'll call her back this afternoon unless you want to. Are you going in to the court today?" The subject changed again.

"Not today, you?"

"Yes, for a couple hours, I think."

After coffee on Monday morning, I sat down with John and gave him the three points I wanted emphasized in the conman concurrence. He took extensive notes, more pages than what I wanted the end product to be, which I pointed out. Length does not equal importance. I spent a half hour going over the revisions to the Waverly opinion. Leslie added two footnotes to respond to points Judy made in the dissent. I wanted to read it over one more time, but I was pretty happy with where we were. There was time for one more cup of coffee before heading to gowning.

We only had a single case to hear today. Luckily it was not one of the marathon oral arguments that the chief was so fond of. This one was a first amendment case. It wasn't as interesting as a newspaper printing something from the CIA that the government thought would get a bunch of spies killed or divulge our nuclear strategy. Nothing that exciting. In this one, a heckler was suing a comedian for slander because the comic was mean to him after the heckler shouted insults during his act at a comedy club. I will grant that the comic questioning the heckler's parentage—a reference to an incestuous relationship between a cinderblock and a brick producing our plaintiff the most printable—was mean, but also funny. But I too questioned his parentage. Not in the same way as the comic but in the shake-my-head did mommy fight all your battles when you were in school manner.

The heckler had lost at both the district and circuit court levels, correctly in my view. Somehow, he found an out-there think tank (dumb tank in my opinion) dedicated to changing the libel and slander rules, to bankroll his legal fees throughout the process. Through those lawyers, he also convinced four justices that this was worth spending our time on. Based on the more than one hundred amici briefs on the table beside my desk, a lot of groups on both sides thought it was important too.

More for amusement than information, I read through some of the friend of the court briefs submitted by the more radical organizations on both sides. I confess here that; no, I did not come close to reading each one on the pile. A group calling themselves the Black Comedians for Profanity submitted a brief that could have been the transcript of an Eddie Murphy or Richard Pryor HBO special. It contained multiple uses of the seven words you can never say on television. I plead guilty that the lawyer and judge in me desperately want to provide a footnote reference to George Carlin here, but will restrain myself.

On the opposite side was a brief from Pastors for the Preservation of Proper Etiquette. I was disappointed they couldn't come up with another "P" word for their name. I spent more time racking my brain for another to complete the alliteration than I did reading the dribble on how public insults should not be protected language and that Don Rickles was a descendant of Satan. If I didn't know they were serious, it would have been almost as funny as the black comedians.

I made a brief pitstop in the men's room, having learned my lesson from the recent argument and knowing that an hour would seem long after the multiple cups of coffee I'd consumed this morning. Gowns on, we shook hands, and proceeded to the bench, fifteen minutes late as the chief had been tied up by some critical administrative matter, he said. Romo leaned over to me and whispered she heard he'd been dealing with whether to add strawberry ripple ice cream to the choices in the court cafeteria. Certainly, something requiring the close attention of the Chief Justice of the United States.

The chief called the case, and the lawyer from the dumb tank arguing for the heckler approached the lectern. It was his first appearance before the court. Just looking at him, I could tell this was not going to go well.

"Mr. Chief Justice, and may it please the court, this morning I am offering prayers to be able to assist this eminent court in understanding the necessity of revisiting the precedents on slander and libel so incorrectly decided..." That was as far as he got before Romo interrupted.

"Prayer isn't a strong argument against precedent that is presumed to be correct absent major error, which is not well substantiated in your brief. It seems like your argument, such as it is, says that saying something like 'your mother wears army boots' should expose the speaker to paying financial damages. Based on playing the dozens on the Brooklyn street corner near where I grew up, I could have won, and lost, millions of dollars under your scheme."

"We would respectfully disagree. The error of the previous decisions is obvious to any..." he was interrupted again.

"You may want to rethink that contention, Mr. Wise," Judy started in from the other end of the bench. His surname was oxymoronic, to be kind. It was time for me to dig into my game. I knew that Perry, Olive Oyl, and Jose would be chiming in shortly, and probably even Romona. This guy was toast.

Fifty-five minutes later, it was mercifully over, although I'm not sure the advocate for the heckler thought there was any mercy involved. Counsel for the comedian had an easy time in her half hour. I suspected this one would be unanimous, although I still did not understand the four votes to hear it in the first place. A lot of our decisions are unanimous. The thirty-odd percent that are 9-0 don't receive anywhere the coverage that the 5-4 ones do.

Judy walked along with me on the way back to our respective chambers. "We're all set for Easter. I talked to Courtney and told her we both were coming. Get that bucket of bolts you drive serviced and make sure it's roadworthy. I don't want to get stuck on the side of the road."

My eight-year-old Honda Civic was a running joke with our kids, and most of the justices as well. The eight others on the court drove vehicles ranging from Mercedes, BMW, and Perry's black Cadillac Escalade; my little and dated sedan stood out in the parking area reserved for the nine of us. Even Judy drove a new Lexus. But my old buddy ran good and I could fit it in parking spaces around town, unlike Perry. And if the body got a scratch or two, I wasn't losing sleep over it. With 175,000 plus miles on it, I was driving it until it died. Dented and dinged, the right rear hubcap missing, a car dealer would charge me to trade it in—okay not really, but I wasn't getting much for it.

"I'm due for an oil change, and I'll check the air in the tires," I said.

"Good, and get the car checked too," Judy joked with far too much enthusiasm as she turned to enter her chambers.

10

The *Waverly* decision was released the middle of the week. Judy and I discussed it and agreed that we would not read either of our opinions from the bench. It was the first decision since Judy's appointment where we were on opposite sides *and* each wrote the so-called lead opinion for our respective positions. We both knew it wouldn't be the last, but there was no reason to draw any more attention to the situation than it was going to get from the court watchers. The chief announced the result and the lineup of justices joining and dissenting.

As expected, there were a couple articles the next day, focused more on Judy and I than the substance of the opinions; unfortunate, but not surprising. Also, as we'd anticipated, that was it and the media went on to other more sensational news the next day. What I hoped, but could not be sure of, was that the next time we wrote conflicting opinions, there would be less attention. And that was on tap when the drone case opinion was finished, unless Judy changed her mind, which I knew from long personal experience, was not going to happen.

Easter was early this year. The drive to our daughter's house took about four hours.

It was great seeing the kids again. I carried in our bags to the separate bedrooms our daughter had arranged. Judy smirked as I put her roller bag in the room. My daughter caught the look, but said nothing, just looked confused.

My baby girl had learned well, and cooked an incredible meal. We all ate too much, and like the old guy I had become, I fell asleep in a big comfortable chair in her family room. I woke up in time for dessert. We all played monopoly after the dishes were cleaned up, like when they were kids, although my son-in-law was new to the tradition.

We were good that night and didn't sneak into each other's room. After breakfast the next morning, I loaded the car for our drive back. My daughter had that same crossed arm look that Judy used on certain occasions.

"My you two are getting along well," she said as I heaved Judy's bag, packed with sufficient clothes for an around the globe cruise instead of our short weekend trip, into the trunk of the car. The ride home was standard for us, similar to many when we were married. The radio was tuned to a soft rock station I abhorred, and she slept while I drove. The minute I tried to turn the radio to ESPN or any other sports channel, she woke up, and slapped my hand away from the dial. Strangely, I enjoyed the familiarity.

Judy's minimal level of consciousness allowed me a degree of light introspection, even if irritated by multiple Christopher Cross songs per hour. What I discerned is these quirks, which previously would have irritated me, okay pissed me off, I now found, if not enjoyable, at least tolerable. And tolerable may even be harsh. I was amused that my attitude was almost Zen-like in the acceptance of that which previously would have infuriated me. Perhaps it was evidence I was mellowing. I'm sure Judy would say it was about time.

Back at the court, we entered the busiest time of the term. We would hear arguments into April, but May and most if not all of June would be devoted to finishing the decisions from those sittings and a number from earlier in the term. The sooner we got done, the sooner we could recess for the summer. And the longer we went into June, the more frustrated we all got with each other.

We'd also get a good percentage of the cases which would be heard the following October slated. Hopefully this would not be one of those years when some rush crisis caused a late term argument and decision. These were usually controversial, and as I've said multiple times, the speed usually produced bad law.

My drone opinion was almost done. Four drafts and a bunch of editing completed; it needed a polish. Baseball season was starting, something I found more interesting than an 8-1 decision. I've heard it said that people who like baseball are boring. Although I consider myself a fascinating fellow, I realize that I'm in the minority holding that opinion. Also, there aren't many Cincinnati Reds fans outside of Ohio, and from the attendance at home games, not even that many there anymore.

I had a half dozen concurrences and dissents in various stages of completion and was considering writing one or two dissents from the denial of cert following our last conference, something I seldom did. The clerks were working their butts off. That was good on multiple levels. I didn't write on every bullshit case that came along just to spell out minor differences with a majority or dissent, so the opinions they worked on were substantive. With few exceptions, the majorities I had were interesting. The volume and diversity of cases gave them a priceless experience. Priceless is probably a bad word choice, as a whole lot of big-name law firms would put a very high price on their experience and I expected them to start asking for an occasional day off starting soon for the inevitable interviews they'd be offered.

I picked up a draft opinion to read through, which showed up in my in-box, the real kind on my desk full of paper, not the computer, this morning. Our resident teetotaler was writing for the majority on a case involving a California winery which got caught substituting plonk, cheap-ass wine they acquired on the bulk market, for a single vineyard labeled cabernet they made most years and charged an arm and a leg for. The fancy label and high price fooled a lot of buyers, but not all. Terrible scores on this normally superb wine by a couple of critics got the attention of a Napa Valley newspaper investigative reporter, fresh out of journalism school, who bought a couple bottles and had them analyzed.

The report moved from the front page of the *Napa Gazette* or whatever it was, to the *New York Times* and *Washington Post,* just to name a few. It showed that instead of being cabernet from the mountain vineyard on the label, for which they got well in excess of $100 a bottle, the bottles contained a cheap blend of a little merlot, cabernet franc, and mostly lesser-known and even less expensive red varietals.

A score of alphabet lettered agencies from the state and feds went after them. There was a recall, refunds, fines, and all kinds of wonderful things that happened to the winery. None of that was what this case was about. In the normal course of doing business and in selling the fake wine, the winery paid a variety of taxes based on the high selling price. With the wine recalled and the bottles that weren't drunk prior to it all poured down the drain, the winery wanted the money they paid in taxes back. The places that had collected it were not inclined to agree, and after some differences of opinion between the district and ninth circuit, we now had it. I was amused to read in the winery's brief that a few wine critics had given the plonk-filled bottles ninety plus numeric scores, consistent with previous years, much to the subsequent embarrassment of those so-called wine experts. How that advanced their argument to recoup their tax money wasn't clear, but lawyers will throw everything against the wall and hope something sticks.

Even after the years I'd spent on the court, tax cases still made my head hurt. Firewater had done yeoman's work in explaining this one so that even I could understand it, and I was inclined to agree with his conclusion that, sorry Charlie, you're not getting a dime back. He did a grand tour through our precedents in arriving there, which I didn't bother to follow in detail, but his rationale was reasonable, and after reading it, sent him my "join" using the strange terminology of the court.

On Friday, with no conference scheduled, we started up 95, jammed into my Honda Civic. Jammed because of the immense amount of space the behemoth Perry took up. He had to sit in the front passenger seat to avoid discharging effluent from the motion sickness that would occur if he rode in the rear, even assuming he might fit.

"Sitting next to me on the team plane, and watching and smelling me fill the air sick bag, was a hazing ritual for the rookies," Perry told us.

That meant Romo, the shortest of the two women by an inch or two, was squeezed into the minimal space remaining behind Perry, since the seat was jammed back as far as it could go. That or amputating the stilts he called legs. Judy got a couple extra inches seated behind me. The two women chatted over some repairs Romo's car needed, and the cost of such services in the DC area for the high-end European brand she drove.

"Olive Oyl told me a long time ago, if it has tires or testicles, it will give you trouble," Romo said.

"Olive Oyl said that," I interrupted, looking in the rear-view mirror.

"Olive Oyl is the Yoda of the female members of the court," Romo said.

"With the voice to prove it," I pointed out. They went back to their conversation, ignoring me.

We were enroute to a contemplative event requiring intellectual rigor…and sunscreen. No, not an outdoor legal conference, although such an event would be an excellent idea, and one, having thought of it, I will raise with the chief judge of the circuit which I am responsible for as a justice. Instead, we would be watching the Philadelphia Phillies taking on the hated New York Mets. Not hated by me, but by diehard Yankee fan, Romo.

The intellectual rigor would be needed to suffer through watching the overpriced free agents signed for ridiculous contracts at the tail end of their careers. Along with the Double A minor league quality pitching staff, which were all they could afford after signing other team's superstars who could now barely make it around the bases if the muscle memory happened to connect bat with ball. That and keeping score on a classic baseball score card, which I insisted on doing.

Luckily, the beer and hot dogs would be good, if overpriced. The weather was perfect, and even a bad game of baseball was preferable to a day reading briefs, so off we went. Not having a time clock to punch, or otherwise account for days off is certainly a job benefit of being a Supreme Court justice.

We made our way carefully to our seats, good ones, halfway up on the lower level behind the third base side dugout. Carefully, because we were carrying our drinks; beer for me, Perry, and Romo, and white wine for Judy. Call me pretentious, but while I can tolerate beer in a plastic cup, a picnic quality riesling in same strikes me as damn near criminal. I comprehend the inherent issues with glass at professional sporting events, especially in the City of Brotherly Love where even Santa fears to tread (I could put another footnote here, but will refrain; you can google it), but when did white wine make it onto the baseball stadium menu? Carefully was particularly operative for Perry as along with his large beer, he carried three hot dogs and a tray of nachos. When he observed me shaking my head as he settled into his seat, he smiled. "No worries, this should get me through the bottom of the second inning."

That was less time than it might sound as the lead-off hitter was walking toward the plate as we sat down. The weekday crowd was sparse; it was a day game and the Phillies were terrible. Occasionally recognized in restaurants in Washington, we were agreeably anonymous here. Even back there, thankfully, a justice's television time was usually limited to an obligatory shot of us sitting on our hands during the President's annual State of the Union address, to avoid any appearance of bias. Other than the two or three hundred viewers that paid attention, most of those watching saw blobs in black robes, not the people in them.

    Here at the ballpark in shorts, t-shirts, and the obligatory cap, mine my ancient and faded Cincinnati Reds hat, we looked like average middle-aged office workers playing hooky for the day, although one of us was halfway between six and seven feet and a solid 280 pounds, not your typical accountant or computer programmer. Even though Judy and I were both from Pennsylvania originally, we didn't get a second glance, and were happy for that.

    Perry and Judy sat side-by-side, and carried on a wide-ranging conversation on art, food, wine, decorating, interspersed with occasional f-bomb laced comments on the poor play of the Phillies—from both. Romo and I commiserated about the chief's lousy assignments as well as the play on the field, with the occasional use of the same coarse language. The Mets were ahead by five runs by the sixth inning and Perry had moved on to cheesesteaks and his third beer. Two hot dogs and a bag of peanuts would hold me through dinner, supplemented by another beer which I nursed. Judy convinced Romo to switch to wine, her acquiescence disappointing to me, but I bit my tongue on the topic of the inappropriate glassware. At least they didn't add ice to the wine, which I considered almost a death penalty criminal offense.

    After the game, we adjourned to the Ritz Carlton hotel downtown where we had rooms booked for the night. Although not optimistic, I did arrange for adjoining rooms for Judy and I. You know, those ones with the two interior connecting doors that haven't been opened since Aunt Sady's wedding party stayed there fourteen years ago.

    The four of us went to dinner at, for me at least, the unreasonable hour of eight that evening. While the hotdogs had been good and reasonably filling along with the two beers at the game, I'd been ready to eat since six.

    Dinner was good. We'd looked for something within walking distance of the hotel. I had a steak, medium rare. Perry had some sort of veal dish, Judy, shrimp scampi. Romo ordered an Italian dish which she critiqued throughout the dinner on the quality of the ingredients, preparation of the sauce, the presentation, and how she would do all of it better. Standard fare when you dined out with Romo. It was one of her hobbies. I'd long joked that she should moonlight for the *Washington Post* writing restaurant reviews.

When we returned from dinner, Perry and I adjourned to the hotel bar, and Judy and Romo went up to their rooms. We each ordered a bourbon over ice and took a dimly lit corner table away from the half dozen people seated at the long dark wood bar. It was nice to get away during the term and enjoy the great American pastime, even a bad version.

"I didn't think a baseball team could play worse than our Nationals, but the Phillies proved me wrong," Perry said.

"Might have been worse if they were playing a good team," I said. The Mets were only three games ahead of them in the National League East standings so far this season.

"So, when are you two going to go public?" Perry made a radical change of the subject.

"What the hell are you talking about?"

"Look, I'm sure the other five are oblivious, but it's pretty clear that you and Judy have something going on. Romo and I have been talking about it. She thinks you look at Judy like a junior high crush. I think it's gone way beyond that."

"Jesus," I said. He just sipped his drink and stared at me. This must've been what the other team's players felt like, those eyes glaring out from behind the facemask of that blue Giants helmet.

"Yeah, well, uh, we're…"

"Look dude, I'm not looking for play-by-play. If you two are hooking up and happy, that's great. Eventually one of the others is going to notice something, is all I'm saying."

"If they do, they do. I don't think any of them are going to call the *Washington Post*," I said.

"So, what's your plan?"

"What do you mean?"

"Harry, you were miserable after the divorce, this last one. You've been entirely different since Judy got to the court. Don't be a dumbass. Marry the girl. Again," he said.

The bourbon caught in my throat and I coughed. Now it was my turn to stare, but more stunned than intimidating. Perry swallowed the rest of his drink, smiled, and stood. He patted me on the shoulder.

"Think about it, Harry. See you in the morning."

In the morning, we all met for breakfast before the drive back.

"I slept great last night," Judy said as we sipped coffee waiting for our respective fried eggs, pancakes, omelet, waffles, or in Perry's case, all of them.

I knew from firsthand experience how well she'd slept. After going up to my room from the bar, I managed to open my half of the connecting doors between our rooms, and tapped lightly on hers. Nothing.

The ride back was different than the trip up. My three companions talked the entire way. When one of them would question my lack of participation I would say "just concentrating on driving." As there was little traffic on the weekend morning, especially compared to what we encountered daily, they weren't buying it, but didn't press me either.

I kept thinking about Perry's comments last night. I don't know about other people, but I don't do deep introspection well, and he had forced me into it. Especially disturbing was how much he was right about. Yes, I was miserable after the divorce, came into the term with low interest in the work and plans to coast through the year. He was also correct that all those things changed after Judy took Judd's seat. My mind worked overtime trying to find another reason that I could assign to those changes other than Judy's presence. The complete lack of success that I had rationalizing various other explanations, well, pissed me off.

The inability to find another logical argument caused the lawyer in me to return to the initial hypothesis. Finally, the judge in me had to interpret the facts and if the outcome was not what I thought it should be, ignore those personal feelings in my ruling. Except all this was all personal feelings, damn it. And then I'd start the process again.

By the time we'd gotten back to the city and I'd dropped each of them off, Judy last, I was ready to rule on the case Perry had presented. I pulled up to the front door of Judy's building. She'd taken Perry's place in the front seat after he extricated his legs, complaining the entire time and insisting that any such future trips would be conducted using his Escalade. Judy leaned over and kissed me on the cheek.

"Thanks Harry, this was a great idea. I had a terrific time." She got out and I retrieved her bag from the trunk. She extended the handle and wheeled it to the door, turned around and waved, and disappeared inside. I got back in the car. It was the first time in my legal career I wasn't sure I was happy to have my ruling upheld.

On Monday, we were back to work. Come 5:00 PM, the group gathered around my table for cocktails and commiserated about the poor Phillies again. With nothing positive to say, the conversation shifted to work.

"You see that weird one in the pile of cert petitions that came in today?" Perry asked.

"A little more specific? There's a bunch of weird ones in there," Romo said.

"The television one," he said.

"Huh?" I said, having not looked at any of them yet.

"This couple is watching this World War I movie and…" Perry began

"World War II," Romo interrupted.

"Whatever, World War II," Perry shot her a look. "And their kid, a baby…"

"Two years old," Romo again.

"Jesus," I said. Judy just smiled at the three of us.

"Anyhow, the kid claps every time they show an American tank and makes raspberry noises when a German one comes on. The video of this goes on that show America's Weirdest Videos…"

"I don't think that's exactly the name," Judy this time.

"Whatever," Perry shoots Judy the same look.

"Amusing, but not hysterical. What's the point?" I asked.

"Anyhow, the point is, some other couple saw it and wanted equal time to show their Nazi baby dressed like a storm trooper, with a little swastika arm band dropping rocks on little green plastic army men, American, I guess. The television people won't put it on, so now there's this First Amendment suit."

"And this got here how?" I start. "Wait, don't tell me, 9th Circuit?"

"You got it," Romo's Brooklyn accent turning the three words into one.

113

A few days after our return from the ball game, Romo strolled into my chambers near the end of the day. She opened my globe, grabbed a glass, some ice, and poured herself a drink.

"Want one?" she asked.

"Well since you're helping yourself to my best liquor, sure I'll join you," I said.

She grabbed another glass, a handful of ice, and poured a generous serving of bourbon over it. Both glasses in hand, she walked over to my table, and sat down taking the chair opposite where she obviously expected me to be seated.

I came around my desk, took my seat like a good boy, and picked up my glass, confused but interested in what was going on.

"Cheers," I said, raising the glass and then taking a swig.

"Back at you," she said, taking a big sip herself.

"What are you doing for dinner tonight," she asked.

"Anything you want," I said. An invitation from Romo was not to be turned down.

"Six at my place," she said, and slammed the rest of her drink back. Without another word, she rose and headed for the door.

I hung around chambers, working on this and that until it was time to leave for Romo's. At five minutes to six, I walked up to her front door, having made a liquor store stop to pick up a bottle of Barbaresco I figured would go well with whatever she might be cooking. Entering, I found Romo in the kitchen, as expected.

"Where's everybody else?" I asked.

"What are you talking about?" She returned my query.

"I don't know. I just assumed Judy and Perry would be here. Are they coming?"

"Nope. Just you and me. Like the old days." Romo and I came on the court about a year or so apart, before both Perry and Judy.

"Oh, okay," I said, a little confused. "What are we having?" I changed the subject.

"Comfort food, babe, spaghetti and meatballs," she said.

Spaghetti and meatballs may strike most as pedestrian food, and coming from someplace other than Romo's, I would agree. The dry spaghetti in a box with grocery store sauce out of a jar that I, and most people, would make on a weekday night was not what we would be dining on, no sir, it was not.

I opened the wine while Romo checked the violently boiling water and added enough salt to turn it into the Pacific Ocean. A towel covered freshly made pasta ready for a short residence in the cauldron. A large pot simmered next to it with a homemade spaghetti sauce which I knew without asking contained only the finest ingredients. The handmade meatballs bathed in the sauce, each exchanging flavor with the other.

Knowing where the important stuff was kept in her kitchen, I went to the cupboard and grabbed two wine glasses and poured each of us a serving of the Barbaresco. There was fresh bread on the counter. I ripped off a small piece and dipped it into the slowly bubbling sauce and popped it in my mouth. A small Italian waving a very large knife shooed me away from the bread.

She dumped the fresh pasta into the boiling water for its short bath. Romo educated me long ago on how little time the homemade stuff took to cook versus the box spaghetti I grew up with. She watched it, pulled one strand out to taste, and deemed it done. With tongs as long as her arms, she grabbed the spaghetti, placed it in a large bowl, and then sauced it to perfection, turning it with the tongs. She grated parmesan cheese on top, added meatballs, and sprinkled some fresh herbs.

We sat at the table in the kitchen, her still wearing her apron, reminding me of meals at my grandmother's house. I had a serving, some fresh bread, and a glass of wine, and watched as she piled another helping on my plate. The eating slowed but the enjoyment did not. At this point, she revealed the reason for the dinner invitation.

"What are you going to do about Judy?" she asked, sitting back staring at me, reminding me even more of my grandmother. Luckily, I was smart enough not to say this out loud.

"Do about what?" I asked, not sure if I knew or liked where this was going.

"She still loves you, dumbass, although I'm not sure why," she said.

"She tell you that?"

"I called you the right name," she shook her head. "No, she didn't tell me. Women don't have to talk about things like that, we know."

"And I'm supposed to do what?"

"I guess that's the operative question. You were miserable after the last divorce. Actually, you were the same after all of them." Romo had a front row seat to my love life for well in excess of a decade.

"Guilty as charged," I said.

"Yes, but since Judy got here, you've been happy again. Question pending is what're you gonna do about it," she said, her Brooklyn accent coming on strong. While it never entirely went away, she could turn it on like being back on the block when she wanted to.

"You're the second one in a week to point that out," I frowned.

"Really," she said. I wouldn't want to play poker with Romo. Her face and body language gave me nothing on whether she knew about Perry's little chat with me.

"Really," I answered. "So, what do you think I should do?" I asked, not knowing for sure if I wanted to know.

"I'm not sure an old maid like me is the best provider of relationship advice. But I remember when I was a prosecutor many moons ago. Patterns convince juries and judges. You're happy when you're married, miserable when you're not, and you've got a woman who for whatever reason, still loves you and seems to make you happy. Looks open and shut to me."

I nodded, and thought about her comments.

"What's for dessert?" I changed the subject.

11

A week or so later near the end of a workday, Judy came into my chambers carrying a legal pad.

"Can you refresh my memory? Is *Hanover* 7-2 or 6-3. I looked back in my notes and it's not clear. I got the joins from everybody I thought I was supposed to except for the chief and Firewater. Since the chief assigned it, I assumed he was voting in the majority. Firewater told me he was going to read it this week, but crickets from the chief," she said. *Hanover v. IRS* was another of the litany of tax cases that made my head hurt.

"Don't worry about it. He does this a couple times a term. He'll vote with the majority, assign the opinion, wait until everyone else is done writing, then ask for a dozen changes in order to join or just switch sides," I explained.

"Shit," she said.

"Yep, and it doesn't matter in this case, but it's a bitch when it's 5-4, especially if you have to negotiate a litany of changes with him and then consult with the rest of your side to make sure those adjustments don't cause them issues."

"How would you handle it in this one if he asked for revisions?" She asked.

"I'd tell him to pound sand. You already have five or six votes for the opinion as it stands. He can concur or dissent, as he sees fit."

"You've done that?" She asked.

"Oh yeah, several times. I don't give a shit about how his academic reputation looks if he joins something I wrote that his professor buddies think is pedestrian. It's just bullshit when he votes with the majority, assigns the opinion, then switches. At least it's only occasional with him. I've heard Warren Burger was renowned to vote however he had to in order to control assigning the opinion, then switch later," I said.

"Great," she said, frowning. She put her pad down to her side.

"Do you want to go out for dinner Saturday?" She asked.

"Sure, pizza or somewhere else?"

"How about someplace fancier? I'm in the mood to go someplace where we eat with a knife and fork," she smiled.

"Sounds good. Where do you want to go?"

"I don't know. Surprise me," she said.

I picked a nice steakhouse. Not Charlie Palmer nice, but a good restaurant. We both enjoyed red meat, me a bit more than Judy, but the choice drew no complaints. They had some seafood on the menu, but that was not the specialty of the house. I perused the wine list while Judy looked at the menu. New York strip, rare or medium rare depending upon how they described their internal temps, was my go-to. A big-ass porterhouse would be nirvana, but only if Judy would split it with me. I could devour that much meat when younger, but no longer.

From the wine list, I picked a merlot from a good California producer, figuring it would go better with the filet mignon I expected Judy to select than a big powerful cabernet would. One great thing I'd always enjoyed about dining with her was as long as there was wine in the glass, she really didn't care what kind or color for that matter, and happily allowed anyone else to choose. The waitress returned and I placed the order for the bottle. Judy, as usual, was still considering her options.

A few minutes passed, all with Judy's face still buried in the menu, and the waitress brought the bottle, opened it, and poured me a taste. I was happy with the choice. Didn't really matter to the restaurant. Unless the bottle was corked, which might happen to me once every couple years, they weren't taking it back even if I didn't care for the wine. And some places, even if it had the musty sulfurous smell and taste of a corked bottle, you were in for an argument. I'd done well with the choice here, though, so I happily nodded to the young lady and she added to my glass and poured for Judy. Finally ready to order, Judy surprised me.

"Do you want to split the porterhouse?" she asked.

"Absolutely," I said. I looked up at the waitress and said "medium rare, please," in deference to Judy preferring her beef not to still be mooing when it reached the table.

We had small salads and fresh bread while awaiting our slab of beef. The restaurant had their timing down. A few minutes after the waitress removed our salad dishes, a crackling platter arrived with the porterhouse carved and returned to the bone, glistening with a light coating of herbed butter. Our plates had baked potatoes with sour cream, and spinach, classic steakhouse fare. I added my spinach to the pile on Judy's plate, content with my meat and potatoes.

To me, the porterhouse is the best of both worlds, part New York strip, part filet. We both took some of each. The richness of the strip flavor contrasted with the tenderness of the filet, and the food and wine made each other better. We chatted as we ate.

"Did you hear anything from the chief on *Hanover* yet?" I asked.

"Yes, he finally wrote me. He said he would join if I moved some text from a footnote into the main body. It's stupid, changes nothing, but I said okay to keep the peace. I talked to Olive Oyl, and she said nobody is going to care, so not to worry about it."

I knew I didn't; I had joined the dissent written by Romo, except for one section I thought was a little harsh.

"Yeah, sometimes I think it's easier to deal with the dissent than the people who supposedly agree with you. I try not to make my vote conditional on a few sentences here and there, but I admit I've done it before. When it's close, a few words can send the teeter totter in the other direction," I said.

"I don't disagree, but in this case, it's just nitpicking shit. I said that to Olive Oyl, and she laughed and explained that the item the chief wanted moved related to a majority he authored about three years ago, and she figured he wanted it more prominently mentioned," I laughed.

"Aah, the plot thickens; yes, gotta impress his fellow professors with his brilliance," I said.

Judy changed the subject. "It's nice how well we've been getting along," she began. I wasn't sure where this was going.

"Definitely," I said.

"Did you think it would be like this when I was appointed?" I finished the chunk of beef in my mouth and washed it down with a big swig of merlot before answering.

"I have to admit I did not," Honesty was the best policy at this point, especially since she would have known immediately if I lied.

The steak was excellent, and it disappeared with the bottle of merlot into our respective stomachs. We split a piece of the flourless chocolate cake for dessert. Judy had a brandy and I had decaf coffee. It was a typical warm May evening in DC, but not too humid. Judy slipped her arm through mine as we walked to my trusty chariot, the Honda having fit into a parking place a larger, fancier car wouldn't have.

"Would you like to come up for a drink, some television, or whatever?" Judy asked as we pulled into the garage at her building. "Whatever" definitely sounded good to me.

"Sure," I said, locating a parking place.

In her condo, Judy made us each a drink while I flipped through the channels, settling on a movie to watch. I knew better than to select the bang bang action movie I would have preferred, settling for a romcom that didn't look insipid. Judy brought the drinks over and settled on the couch with me, pleased with the choice.

We sipped and watched and watched and sipped. I might have dozed for a few minutes here and there. I paid about as much attention to the movie as I do oral argument, my thoughts elsewhere, although in the case not a game on my phone.

When the credits were scrolling down the screen, I made up my mind. Time to see if the advice I'd been getting was right. I put my glass down, rose, and stretched a hand out to Judy. She took it, and stood up as well.

"How about we move on to 'whatever,'" I said, leading her toward the bedroom. She smiled, nodded, and followed me down the short hallway. Maybe they *are* right, I thought.

I woke up in the morning to the smell of coffee and bacon. I can't think of a better aroma on a Sunday morning. I hit the bathroom, got dressed, and followed my nose toward those incredible smells.

Judy must've gotten up much earlier. She was showered, dressed, and had a full breakfast ready to go onto the table. Fresh squeezed orange juice, coffee, eggs over easy, home fries, bacon, and wheat toast. My all-time favorite morning meal. One I would get in a diner maybe twice a year; okay four times. I grabbed her and planted a kiss on her.

"This is awesome," I said.

"I remember what you like," she said. We dug into the feast she'd prepared. I knew I wouldn't be eating lunch today.

"What do you have planned for the day?" Judy asked. Now I was concerned, wondering if she wanted me to do something with her.

"Going to the Nationals game with Perry," I said. She brightened. Concern returned, and confusion.

"That's great," she said. Now curiosity.

"What're you doing?" I asked.

"Shopping with Romo, then a late lunch with her and Olive Oyl," she said.

"Nice," I said, although it was hard to imagine Olive Oyl as a scintillating lunch companion, especially with the two of them.

I got home with plenty of time to shower and shave before meeting Perry at the ballpark. The game day weather was perfect. My Cincinnati Reds hat in this crowd was not. I heard a few boos as we walked to our lower deck seats, me with a beer, Perry with nachos, two hotdogs, plus his own beer, which I guessed would get him into the second inning. We settled into our seats having stopped on the steps for the anthem, and watched the Nationals take the field. The lead-off hitter walked to the plate. Perry leaned over to me.

"Heard you had a good night," he said.

"How the fuck? Do you work for the goddamn CIA?" I said, too loudly. I looked around and luckily all the fans sitting close enough to hear were happily watching the first Reds batter strike out. Perry laughed.

"I'm like those investigative reporter dudes. I never reveal my sources," he said. I was fuming. A little.

"As long as I don't read about it in the damn *Post*," I said, quieter this time. He laughed again and inhaled half a hotdog. The Reds second batter lined out to short.

I calmed down, enjoyed the game, and even ate two hotdogs and had a second beer myself. Compared to the four dogs, the tray of nachos, a bag of peanuts, two slices of pizza, and three beers Perry consumed during the nine innings—a light day for him—I was a piker. More than the food, the Reds winning 3-2 made my day. We adjourned to a small bar a block from the stadium to let the traffic abate.

With two much less expensive beers in hand, we found a small table against the wall.

"It's a great time of year, Harry. Closing in on the end of the term, the humidity hasn't set in yet, and love is in the air," he said with a big grin, raising his glass.

"You're an asshole," I said. He just smiled more.

"Be that as it may," he said.

"All I'm going to say is you might be right," I hedged.

"Hey, I sense progress. I'll take it," he said, signaling the bartender for two more beers.

Back in chambers on Monday, it was a busy day. I worked on my remaining majorities, dissents, and concurrences, and read through drafts of those by the rest of the justices. Tuesday was much the same, except for reviewing cert petitions as well. We were closing in on Memorial Day and getting all the remaining decisions issued by the end of June. The earlier the better, in my opinion. On Wednesday, I had pretty much made up my mind.

In the afternoon, I walked over to Judy's chambers. She was busy too, piles of file folders and printed draft opinions covering her desk, admittedly in a more organized fashion than mine. She looked up when I entered.

"How about pizza on Friday?" I asked.

"Sure, the regular place?" She asked.

"Of course," I said.

"Okay," she said.

"I'll get us a table," I said, and headed back to my piles of paper.

The rest of the week went normally. Working through the opinions was drudgery, frustrating, and sometimes irritating when on the losing side of a 5-4 decision you thought was important. Friday couldn't come soon enough, and at the same time, arrived too fast. I was nervous.

"So, I was wondering. What would you think of getting married?" I asked, after we'd ordered and following an extra-large swig of wine and a deep breath, sweat running down my neck under my collar even with the air conditioning.

"To who?" She laughed

"Uh, me."

"Do you have a diamond in your pocket there?"

"Don't you still have the one I gave you the first time?" I asked.

"Yes, of course."

"Well…"

"You cheap bastard," she laughed. She was enjoying this way too much.

The pizza arrived, temporarily relieving me from my misery. With the triangular metal server, I slid slices onto each of our plates to cool. I took another big slug from my wine glass, wishing it was something stronger. This was way easier the first time.

We each ate two slices in silence. I racked my brain on what to say next. Of course, I'd be happy to buy her a new ring, but how should I work that into the conversation now? I looked over. Judy was staring at me, smiling, and chewing at the same time. The lightbulb finally came on that she was enjoying my utter discomfort.

Finally, she decided to let me up. She put down the slice she was working, took a sip of wine, and began again.

"Yes, I still have the ring," she repeated.

She unbuttoned the top two buttons of her blouse. I got nervous and began looking around the restaurant. Reaching in, she pulled up a long thin gold chain that was around her neck, which I hadn't noticed. At the bottom, with the chain through it, was the engagement ring. She undid the chain, slipped the ring off.

"I have to say, Harry, you were much better at this the first time around," she said, handing me the ring.

I took the ring, looked at it, and then up at her. Reaching over with my other hand, I grasped her left one and slipped the ring on her finger. It fit just like the first time.

I guess I'm living proof that practice does not make perfect," I said.

"Oh, you're such a jerk," she said. "But I'll marry you again anyway."

She wasn't wrong.

While we finished the pizza, our waiter unexpectedly appeared at the table, a large plate in one hand and a bottle in the other. A young busboy accompanying him set flutes in front of each of us while we both looked on in confusion. He set the plate, almost a platter, filled with cannolis, a lit candle jammed in the center. He then presented a bottle of Prosecco, and unbidden, poured glasses for each of us.

"What's this?" I said, still confused.

"Pardon me sir, but I overheard your conversation with the lady. We want to wish you happiness and good things," the waiter said.

"Thank you so much," Judy said, lifting her glass and enjoying a big sip.

"You're quite welcome," the waiter said, "and may I be the first to congratulate you, Mr. and Mrs. Justice."

12

Judy sat on the couch in my chambers while I got both kids on the speaker phone at the same time. After a minute or so of small talk, I got right to the topic at hand.

"I wanted to invite you two the last weekend in June. I'm getting married again."

"Who's the lucky girl this time, and is she at least older than me?" my daughter asked. The sarcasm dripped from the speaker.

"Yes, she's definitely older than you," I answered, enjoying myself.

"Have I met her?" My son asked.

"You certainly have."

"Wait, how did he get to meet her and I haven't?" My daughter protested.

"You've met her too," I said.

Dead silence. After thirty seconds, my daughter chimed in again.

"I can't even begin to think which blonde bimbo this is," she said. My daughter got her snarkiness from me.

"She's not blonde," I said.

"Okay, we're done here. Who is it?" My son got straight to the point, that aspect of his personality from Judy.

"It's your mother," I said.

"Cut the shit, Dad. I'm not calling some blonde, or in this case brunette or red headed chick 'Mom,'" my daughter said.

"No," I said. "Your Mom and I have decided to get remarried."

"Oh, sweet Jesus, have you two lost your freaking minds?" My son asked.

"Possibly, but that's what we're going to do, and we'd like you to be maid of honor and best man, uh, in accordance with your sexes, of course," I said.

I looked over at Judy who had tears streaming down her face, bent over holding her stomach, she was laughing so hard, as she listened to the conversation.

After I hung up, our discussions continued.

"We need to agree on housing as part of this," Judy said.

"We have one too many. What's your point?"

"My place is too small for us and your place is, well your place. I want our place."

"And what does our place look like?"

"I like the brownstone style and being in the city. I want a bigger kitchen than what you have; not Romo size, but something nice. And a living room set up for movies, television, sports, cozy, but that we can have a few people over. What would you want?" She asked.

"I'm fine with those. Three bedrooms would be good for visits from future grandchildren." Another hint. "Maybe a small backyard. I don't want a lot of grass to cut."

"Would you settle for two?" Judy asked.

"Two grandchildren, sure," I said.

"Bedrooms, I meant," she said, shaking her head.

"I guess, but we'd have to stack them like cordwood in there," I grinned. She ignored me.

"One other thing," I had what to me was an important thought. "We need a library, office type room. Lined with bookshelves but big enough for two desks. I don't want to share."

"Yeah, that's a good idea," she said.

"And the room needs to be big enough that the desks aren't against each other. I don't want to sit there, desk to desk, looking at you like we're in the third grade, and I'm sure you don't want to be staring at me if we're both trying to work," I said. She laughed.

"Okay, true, you put the desks however you want them."

"I know one other thing that will change in a new house together," I said, trying to make my eyebrows move in what I hoped would be perceived as a lascivious manner.

"Do tell," she said, her tone telling me I'd been successful although stupid looking, I'm sure.

"I won't have to eat peanut butter and jelly every day for work,"

She threw the pen in her hand at me, just missing my head.

I went to see the chief justice. Okay, that's not chronologically correct. First, I requested an appointment. A justice did not just stroll into the chambers of Chief Justice Palmetto like they do mine. Steeling myself before entering his chambers, I opened the door, and walked in to find him working at his desk, suit coat, if one could call it that, in place. It was a plaid of some sort, red, purple, yellow, and others. It looked like someone had taken the seconds from a Scottish kilt factory and made a suit for the chief. I was glad I'd prepared myself before entering as it kept my reaction to a smile which he could interpret as me being happy to see him rather than laughing out loud as I otherwise would have.

"Good morning, David," I said. If anyone had called him Dave, it was probably back in grade school, if then.

"Good morning, Harry. Good to see you. What can I do for you?" He rose from his desk. Adding the pants to the jacket, it was damn near blinding, especially with the pink shirt and yellow tie.

"I have some news I wanted to share with you," I began. His eyes widened, and he frowned. This time of year, the only reason a justice wants to share news with the chief involves his or her retirement from the court. I was going to enjoy this.

"Have a seat, Harry. I hope you're not about to tell me what I think you are. You're too young, vibrant, too valuable to the court to leave us," he said.

"No, David, it's not that," I said, sitting down on a leather couch he had along a wall of bookshelves. He took a chair opposite me. The chief's chambers were about half again as large as mine.

"Thank goodness. Well then, what is it and can I be of any assistance?" He asked.

"Possibly. What I'm going to share with you might be surprising, but I need to emphasize, is confidential for the time being," I began. He frowned again.

"As you know, I've been married a few times. Judith my first, followed by a couple others…" Now he was getting worried. I could see his eyes whirling around like a slot machine, thinking about news he might have seen about me being in the company of this or that woman. I could tell he was coming up blank.

"…and will be doing so again here shortly, as soon as we can get the term completed. We don't want to interrupt or distract from that work," I said.

"Well, yes, that is prudent and appreciated, Harry. Who is the lucky lady this time?" He asked, dreading the answer, I could tell.

"The good news, David, is you already know her," I said. He now looked confused.

"Really," he sat back, but calmer, knowing he wasn't acquainted with too many young blonde bimbos, which is what he associated me with.

"The bad news, and I hesitate to characterize it that way, may result in you being asked a few questions, but nothing, I'm sure, you won't handle with complete aplomb," I said, smiling. Now we had a facial expression somewhere between concerned and curious. I would love to get the chief into a game of high stakes poker sometime. Unfortunately, I had extracted as much amusement as I was going to get, so I continued.

"You might be asked about court function and some similar issues because…Judith and I have decided to get remarried."

Now he looked like I'd hit him between the eyes with a baseball bat.

"Well, I say, congratulations. That is something. My, I don't think there has ever been two justices married to each other. Things to think about. Rare indeed…" He was babbling now.

"Yes, a unique situation, to be sure, but one which I'm confident we're well equipped to handle," I said.

"My, we'll have to let the President know," he said. I had anticipated that and was ready to head him off.

"Judith will be calling her today as she was her appointee," I said, making it clear he wasn't going to be the one sharing the news.

"Yes, that would be best," he frowned and reluctantly agreed. He loved to call the President.

"There's one other thing we should cover," I said. The mixed confused concerned look returned. God, I needed to get him to the poker table.

"Certainly," he said, encouraging me to continue.

"We're planning to have the wedding ceremony here at the court," his eyes lit up with an assumption I knew I was going to have to spoil.

"Justices Jacobs and Romaldini will be conducting the ceremony, but we would like you and the rest of the brethren to attend. It will be a very small wedding," I said.

"I wouldn't miss it," he said, his face looked like the character Droopy from the old Saturday morning cartoons, understanding he wouldn't be officiating.

I rose to leave, reached over, and shook hands with him. I had to know.

"Great looking suit, David. Wherever did you find it?" I asked.

"An old friend of mine; judge in Britain introduced me to a tailor he knows in Scotland. Marvelous work, don't you think?"

"Yes, it's truly…amazing," I said, not able to get any other positive word to come out of my mouth associated with the ensemble he wore. "I've taken up enough of your time this morning. I'm sure we'll be talking soon," I said and headed for the exit.

"Again, congratulations, and please extend my best wishes to Judy as well," he said as I turned to close the door.

I nodded. Judy would be pissed she'd missed the entertainment.

When it came to gossip around the court, confidential wasn't in the chief's vocabulary. Word promptly spread throughout the building. So far it hadn't leaked to the press. That wouldn't last, we both knew. I sat in Judy's chambers as she placed a call to the president. She was kind enough to do it on speaker phone so I could enjoy the entire conversation.

It took a few minutes, but the president was available and came on the line. The process was eased by Judy emailing the White House chief of staff before I went to see the chief, asking when it might be convenient to have a brief telephone conversation with the President. I'm sure fearing that her first Supreme Court nominee was ready to pack it in already, a call was arranged for the same afternoon.

"Madam Justice, Judith, it's so good to hear from you," the President opened.

"Thank you, Madam President, good speaking with you too. I wanted to share some news before you heard it elsewhere," Judy began.

"Oh, Judith, don't tell me that miserable ex-husband of yours is driving you out of there. Just say the word and I can talk to the Speaker about impeachment," the President said as a horrified look came over Judy's face. You couldn't wipe the grin off mine.

"No, Madam President, quite the opposite, actually, Harry's been fine."

"Oh, thank goodness, so what is this news then?" the President asked.

"I wanted to share that I will be getting married at the conclusion of the term."

"That's wonderful. Who's the lucky man, Judith?"

"Justice Cashman," Judy said.

"Yes, I know you're Justice Cashman. I appointed you," It was turning into Abbott and Costello and "Who's on First." The President sounded a bit condescending.

"No, Madam President, I'm marrying, or should I say, remarrying Justice Cashman." We were up to "what's on second" and heading to "I don't know's on third." I was enjoying this.

"Harry? But you told me he…" The horrified look came back on Judy's face. I stifled my laughter as Judy interrupted the President of the United States.

"Harry's right here, and would love to say hello, isn't that right, Harry?"

"Good afternoon, Madam President," I hollered across the room. I had no intention of getting out of my comfortable seat.

"Oh, Justice Cashman, both of you, I guess congratulations are in order," she said. Yes, we were on third base. She took the conversation back to Judith. "Please let me know when you decide on a date, Judith. I must send you something."

"I certainly will Madam President. Thank you for your time," Judy said.

"Glad to hear from you. Good bye to you both," the President said.

"Good bye, Madam President, please give my regards to the Speaker when you talk to him," I couldn't resist. The telephone clicked off. I looked at Judy.

"That went well," I said, straight faced. She burst into laughter.

After the inevitable leak, and confirmation from Veronica in public affairs, a rabid far right-wing Congresswoman, Maryann G. Taylor from the income tax-free state of Florida, announced the introduction of a bill to impeach both of us. I found it amusing, Judy, less so. For what crime seemed a little unclear to me, and apparently to the other 434 members of the house, as well, since no cosponsors joined. Other than that, the reaction from the legislative branch was muted. One or two commented on taking a "wait and see" approach to if we suddenly started voting together. These individuals had obviously never been married.

The President sent Judy and I, mostly Judy I'm sure, two dozen red roses and a congratulatory note, which of course included a signed picture of her and Judy at the announcement of her nomination. Judy had the note framed, and I made my first marital pronouncement, luckily to no resistance, stating I didn't care where she put it as long as it wasn't in our new shared office at the future home.

13

The thing I most dreaded each term was an emergency petition right when we were trying to wind things up. Inherently, these involved something controversial, and arguably important, at least to someone. The one thing that we, the Supreme Court justices, were not good at was combining important with speed. And I wanted this term over with, pronto.

One of the motley online news sites received a leak of material from NASA or more accurately, somebody who hacked into NASA. The initial information that they teased said that the hacker had used one of NASA's huge space orbiting satellites or telescopes and found life on another planet. It was all convoluted and confusing, with the limited information they released to draw attention to the story. NASA, the Justice Department, and the Pentagon all got together and went to court for an order to restrain the publication of anything further. The news people, naturally, opposed this, and the legal dispute promptly became as much of the story as life on Mars or wherever they thought it was.

The district court and the DC circuit both promptly punted the ball, and we wound up with it on the twenty-yard line, up against our endzone. With the judges of the circuit court declining to do anything, the government filed for an emergency stay with the chief justice. The circuit court knew exactly what they were doing and what was going to happen. Thanks guys, I thought. It was just what we wanted to see on June 2nd as we tried to wind down our term.

Since it came via the DC Circuit it went to the chief, as mentioned, who traditionally supervised them like I did the 3rd Circuit. He issued an emergency stay to prevent publication until the motion could be considered by the full court. That was normal, and no indication of how he or anybody else might vote on the substance of the dispute. By our rules, emergency petitions required five votes to grant cert rather than the usual four.

The chief requested our presence the following afternoon for a conference to discuss whether to continue to stay publication and secondly whether to grant cert and hear the case on an emergency basis. Or we could hold off until October, send it back to the circuit directing them to do their job, or just let the media publish.

If we didn't halt publication, there was no reason to hear the case. We could also halt it, as noted, until October, which would be good for my vacation—and other--plans, but not much else. Seemed irresponsible to me, as reluctant as I was to delve into this so quickly. In the meantime, we would get to read what the reporters had and what the government thought could happen if the material was released to the public.

The chief, at his paranoid best, had directed that the materials should be restricted to the justices alone. Naturally, as soon as they came in, I had Edith make copies for each clerk, and told them to figure on a long night. Edith arranged for pastries and coffee to be delivered at 9:00 AM the next morning when I wanted to walk through everything with the four of them.

I jammed my copy of the file in my briefcase, violating another of the chief's strictures against removing the materials from the building, along with half a peanut butter and jelly sandwich that I hadn't gotten around to eating after all this hit the fan, and told the kids I'd see them in the morning. Their work area had three recently delivered pizza boxes, evidence that by this time in the term they had their priorities straight. I thought about grabbing a slice on my way out the door, but decided to be good.

I spent the evening reading about the possibility of little green men deduced from the presence of oxygen and hydrogen on a rock in some distant galaxy. UFOs that could just as easily be some Soviet space junk that had made its way past Pluto and out of our solar system over the fifty plus years it had been up there.

The observations weren't even close to the sophistication of Hubble much less Webb, not surprising I guessed, since the telescope in question was really there for the Pentagon and supposed to be looking at Chinese tanks, not some rock in the next galaxy over designated XFV13Z, for little green men. That we had the capabilities in space to monitor our near-peer adversaries, and everybody else for that matter, wasn't a surprise to me, and shouldn't be to anybody else who could read above the fifth-grade level. More interesting to me was that nobody seemed to know who hacked into the system and turned it around to look the opposite direction, which I would have thought more important than what we were dealing with. Tomorrow would be interesting.

The next morning, Friday, the clerks and I settled in with coffee and a selection of pastries. The cheese Danish was my favorite, and I made sure I grabbed two from the platter. I briefly summarized the issues then turned the youngsters loose. They were split right down the middle. John took the lead on one side and Leslie the other. To my surprise, Leslie was willing to give the government the benefit of the doubt, hear the case, and likely prohibit publication on national security grounds. John, on the other hand, thought the government hadn't even come close to the threshold necessary to prevent publication.

I withheld my opinion, and just listened, wanting to hear them debate. I would rather encounter a compelling argument in chambers than in conference. It was refreshing to see their passion but respect for the views of the others. It was fun to watch John and Leslie spar with the other two guys nodding along with their respective sides. Don't get me wrong; they were good clerks too, just not as vocal as Leslie and John.

At lunchtime, I ate my peanut butter and jelly sandwich while reading through the government's submission again. My diet was getting a bit redundant, having finished the half sandwich last night for dinner. I closed the folder, folded up my paper lunch bag and stuck it in my briefcase. Putting on my suitcoat, I nodded at the clerks as I headed out of chambers for the conference room, sensing that they were confused. I hadn't given them any hint of my opinion during our discussion or more accurately, their debate.

We took our seats around the large rectangular wood table. I opened my leather portfolio and unscrewed my pen, posting the cap to the back of it and laying it on the yellow pad. For once, my prayers, such as they are, were rewarded. The chief didn't have enough time or material to prepare his normal forty-five-minute lecture. After a ten-minute summary, still more than we needed, he indicated his vote would be to grant, and stay publication until we reached a decision. However, he didn't signal where he was on the substance, which surprised me. Olive Oyl also voted to grant cert, but she seemed to lean against the government's contentions. I was next.

"I would deny and lift the stay. I don't believe they've found little green men, but there's also nothing here that's going to hand China or Russia anything they didn't already know," I said, adding my vote to the tally I had started on the pad in front of me.

It was four to four when it reached Judy. On an ordinary case, her vote wouldn't have mattered, but with the rules on emergency petition cert grants, we would go wherever she took us.

"I'm not convinced by the government's position at this point," she started. I was happy. We could get this term concluded on time. After all, we had something kind of important to do. "But with four of you desirous of hearing argument, I'm willing to go along to give all parties the opportunity to fully air their claims."

"Shit," I said, initially not knowing I'd said it out loud. Luckily only Romo heard, which I knew when she kicked me under the table. The chief concluded the discussions.

"Unless there is some objection, we'll schedule oral argument for next Wednesday and call for any briefs by the end of the day on Monday."

Great. That gave us all of one day to read the last-minute submissions. I hoped the lawyers who would be arguing were smart enough to get us their briefs by Sunday but I had no doubt that paper would be flowing in the door until the close of business on Monday.

Within hours after the decision to proceed and the schedule announced, a snowstorm of paper descended on the court. The most important ones I wanted to read, when they arrived, would be those from the Solicitor General, the firm for the defendant, and any we would get from the intelligence community, CIA, DIA, etc. I had no intention of spending time on those from absolutist first amendment advocates, freedom of the press organizations, right wing shoot-the-reporter groups, and the like. They weren't going to make any arguments I hadn't already thought of and there wasn't going to be time to wade through every page in the pile on my table which was increasing in height every hour.

With the speed at which the briefs arrived, I wondered how much was fresh work and, more likely, how much was recycled cut and paste from previous briefs written on the subject of prior restraint. I asked the clerks to go through as many as they could. Though unlikely, there might be a nugget in one of them. Even dividing the total by four, I had no confidence there would be eyes on every brief submitted before Wednesday. If they found anything unusual or particularly, persuasive, they were to bring it to my attention. With the rushed timelines, it was the best and most efficient thing we could do. It was going to be a long weekend.

At the normal close of business, Judy, Romo, Perry, and I gathered as usual for our Friday cocktail. Unlike most of our end of week gatherings, work was part of the conversation. Perry and Romo were approaching the information inundation pretty much the same way I was. Judy, on the other hand, was trying to read everything that came in the door, a function of her newness on the court.

"Your eyes are going to fall out of your head by Wednesday, baby," Perry told her. Romo nodded, and I kept my advice to myself.

"I'm sure you're right. I just don't want to miss something important," she said.

"It's counterintuitive, but you'll have less of a chance of missing something in a situation like this if you delegate to your clerks. They'll bring you the important stuff, and some that isn't, but you'll be able to focus instead of just scan," Romo said. This time I nodded, while sipping my drink.

"Maybe," Judy said. If she were talking to the kids or me, "maybe" would be a definite "no' but in this case probably meant she was considering it. I could tell she wasn't convinced, though. That said, I knew she would be more receptive to advice from Perry and Romo than me. I guessed that by Sunday morning, she'd either have taken the advice or be a frazzled mess.

I headed home around seven. On my way out, I told the clerks to make sure they were gone no later than eleven. If I'd said nothing, they'd have stayed all night. Saturday and Sunday would be long enough. The more important briefs would start arriving by Sunday night. The court administrator's folks would be in all weekend to keep pushing paper out to our respective chambers. This case didn't warrant any all-nighters in my opinion, regardless of what any of the other brethren were doing. I figured if I told them eleven, there was a chance they'd leave by midnight. I could see the lights on beneath the door to Judy's chambers. Smiling, I shook my head, assuming those lights would still be on tomorrow morning when I arrived.

Acting on my suspicion, I stopped at Dunkin on my way in and picked up two large coffees. Walking down the hallway, sure enough, the lights were still shining from beneath the door in her chambers. I opened it and walked in. The clerks looked like the living dead with paper strewn across every horizontal surface. The guys had more than a full day of beard growth except for one fellow who looked twelve, but even he had sprouted some peach fuzz.

"She in there?" I asked.

"Yes sir," one of the zombies mumbled.

"Rise and shine," I said opening the door and entering her chambers. I tried to exude cheerfulness. Judy was seated behind her desk, holding her head with both hands as she read. She looked up and saw the steaming large Dunkin coffee.

"Bless you," she said, and came around the desk in her stocking feet, wearing sweat pants.

"You knew I'd still be here." It was as much a statement as a question.

"I had a high degree of confidence," I said, sipping my coffee.

She laughed and took a big swig of hers. "I'm beginning to think the three of you were right. We can't keep this up until Wednesday," she said.

"I never said a word," I protested, with a smile on my face, I suspect.

"You didn't have to," she said.

"We all learned the same way. I assume you remember my all-nighters the first year or so."

She nodded, gulping more coffee. "I wonder if I can get this intravenously. As soon as I finish this and wash my face, I'm calling the clerks in and we're switching to your method."

"I'm sure they'll appreciate it. I'll let you get back at it," I said, and turned to leave.

The barrage of paper continued throughout the weekend. By Sunday night, nearly three hundred amici briefs were scattered across the clerk's desks and my round table. The clerks each brought me a few excerpts, most of them amusing more than useful. They had caught on that I enjoyed seeing those.

I left for home around eight, having spent the day reading more of the raw materials that had been leaked, but not yet printed, and whatever the clerks brought me. Nothing in those documents was changing my mind. What I still hadn't seen was the 'who' behind the repositioning of the telescope, satellite, whatever you wanted to call it.

At nine, my phone rang. It was Leslie.

"The briefs from the Solicitor General's office, Pentagon, NSA, and some other intelligence agencies just arrived, sir," she said.

"Great. Go home, and tell the guys the same thing. We'll all read those tomorrow and discuss them in the afternoon."

"Yes sir, I'll relay the message," she said. I had no doubt they would ignore me and were ordering pizza before I put the phone down, so they could start in on those briefs tonight.

The next morning, two of the four of them were at their desks, bleary eyed, which made me wonder if they had even left. Before I could say anything, the other two arrived, looking not much better than the first ones. I grinned at the haggard group.

"I'm guessing you're all ahead of me reading the government stuff. I'll start on it this morning. Let's sit down after lunch and talk through it. And by the way, when I leave tonight, you're all leaving with me. Got it?" A mixture of relief and consternation washed across their faces, but they all nodded.

The day went quickly. I had Edith order sandwiches for everybody from the court cafeteria, a change from the diet of warm and cold pizza the clerks had been living on. We all ate and read and vice versa. The briefs from the Solicitor General's office and the alphabet agencies all read the same. They obviously coordinated with each other. That's not a criticism. If I were the solicitor general, it's what I would have insisted upon. Daylight between any of them would be jumped on by the respondents, and one or more of us, though it would have been helpful to read something new or different.

About two in the afternoon, I was done and called the clerks in. They were as coordinated as the government lawyers, taking the same seats as always.

"Who wants to start?" I asked. Nobody jumped in so I used the school teacher method.

"Leslie, tell me what the government contends and what I should think about it."

She leaned forward in her chair, and took a glance down at her notes.

"The government writes that release of the information will give away sources and methods and claims that anything and everything captured by the telescope or satellite or whatever it is, is classified top secret. They also state that the claims that the pictures and data show life on other planets and alien spacecraft are incorrect."

"Anybody got anything different or more from their reading?" I looked at the four of them. They all shook their heads no.

"So, what should I think? Is the government right?"

"No sir, I don't think so, I've changed my mind," Leslie continued.

"So, you think they did find little green men and Klingons flying around out there?" I joked.

She blushed. "No sir, I don't think the government substantiated their claim that the disclosure will reveal sources and methods. I'm no expert, but I didn't see anything in the documents on capabilities of the telescope that I didn't know or suspect the US could do. And if it didn't surprise me, I'm sure the Chinese and Russians know."

"In reality then, we don't even need to read the respondent briefs when they get here tomorrow," I smiled. Leslie laughed softly.

"I know you're kidding, Justice Cashman, but you're also right. The government, in my opinion, didn't come close to the threshold to stay publication, so no matter what the respondents write, it won't, or at least shouldn't, harm their case." Ever the lawyer, she had to insert a qualifier.

"Any of the rest of you have a different view?" Again, three shaking heads.

"You know what I want to know that the government hasn't told me and I haven't seen in any of the so-called secret materials or other briefs?" I looked at the four of them. One of the quiet ones surprised the hell out of me.

"Who did it," he said. I pointed at him.

"Exactly. Who hacked into a supposedly secure top-secret system and turned a telescope around to look for aliens. This is like right out of an episode of *Big Bang Theory*. Kind of an important question. Even the media, when they do talk about it, has it buried three quarters of the way down the article."

We talked around a few peripheral issues and by the time we were done, it was close to five.

"Alright folks, pack your bags or whatever you take home with you. We're out of here." I hadn't even taken my peanut butter and jelly out of my briefcase. I knew what dinner again tonight would be. I walked out to their bullpen.

"Let's go, you're all leaving." I lined them up like first graders carrying their lunch boxes, or in this case high-end computer backpacks, ready for school dismissal. I wasn't taking a chance that one, or more of them, would stay if I left first. I herded them out the door.

"Have a good night and I'll see you tomorrow," I said.

The next morning, everyone, myself included, looked more chipper, and for the male clerks, shaved. The restorative power of ten hours of sleep is amazing. The brief from the respondents arrived about the same time as the first pot of coffee. The amici briefs continued to pour in; law school professors and other academics getting into the act. It would allow the professors to say "I told the Supreme Court x, y, or z in my brief…" We were so far past the saturation point, I doubted many of those from now until close of business would get more than ten minutes each, if they got that much.

The important one, from the respondent, said what I thought it would. That the prior restraint of publication by the government wasn't justified. While they took an almost absolutist view that I didn't agree with, they made a good showing on the weakness of the government position. What this brief was also silent on was the question becoming more important in my mind. The *who*. Not a surprise as they wouldn't willingly give up their source.

Tuesday was busy again, but for different reasons. The clerks plowed through the remaining friend of the court briefs and put together a bench memo and proposed disposition for me. I worked on fine-tuning my outstanding opinions, majorities, dissents, and concurrences. Drone, as we'd come to call that case around chambers was, and had been pretty much done for a month or more. I'd hung onto it to release it in the June push where an 8-1 opinion would receive less media attention. It would still get some as I wrote the majority and Judy was the sole dissenter, but not as much as it would have gotten pre–Memorial Day.

Finally, it was Wednesday, finally. Hopefully nothing else would get in the way of finishing the outstanding cases and we could conclude the term. That's not to say some huge controversy requiring our attention wouldn't arise in July or August, but historically those are slow months.

We went through our formalities, took our seats, and the chief justice called the case. It was slated for two hours, more than I wanted but at least it wasn't one of the four-hour endurance contests the chief loved.

The solicitor general rose and opened traditional manner.

"Thank you, Mr. Chief Justice, and may it please the court…"

I had my phone with me, but knew I probably wouldn't get too much game time. The solicitor general didn't get too far before she was interrupted.

"Let's cut to the chase, General, why should we accept the government's contention that top secret material, sources and methods will be revealed if we don't permanently stay publication, when there's nothing in the record and your submissions that I haven't read about months ago in the *Washington Post*. I'm not talking about little green men, we'll get to that, I'm talking capabilities," Perry opened the bidding.

"Justice Jacobs, I would disagree with the premise of your question. Our brief shows the critical capabilities of the satellite could be compromised and without publicly divulging…"

"I guess that's a problem then. Our precedents set a high bar to stay publication and restrict freedom of the press, and I don't believe you've come within a country mile of it in this case," Romo raised the bid, pushing in a massive pile of chips.

I smiled. The solicitor general was a highly experienced advocate. She had argued dozens of cases before us in this and previous terms, and she knew she was in trouble. The look on her face showed it. She knew that when Perry and Romo were on the same side, it was all but over. She got a little help from Firewater, but not much, as he pawed through the pile of papers in front of him.

"Do I understand that the government disagrees with the conclusion the respondent reaches or at least reports, that when oriented to outer space, alien life was discovered?" The question had nothing to do with the yes or no question of whether the information could be published, but it gave her a chance to breathe. She was just happy to be able to agree with something coming from the bench.

"Yes, Justice Freehawk, you are correct. The data obtained does not support a conclusion of life on the body identified or the object noted to be a spacecraft. That does not mean that at some time in the future…" Now she was filibustering.

"Two questions, General," I cut her off. "First, the critical item to me is not are there or aren't there little green men out there. It's why we should agree to stay the publication of the information. Being wrong about aliens isn't grounds. People have written about that as far back as the 1800s. And I too am not convinced you've come anywhere near the threshold necessary in your national security concerns…"

"Justice Cashman, I think…"

"I'm not done, my second question is likely no more germane than the Klingons or whoever the respondents think are flying around out there, but I think it's worth asking. And that's who? Who turned the telescope or satellite or whatever it is around? To me that's the national security concern we should be worried about." I sat back to murmurs, both on the bench and in the gallery.

"Uh, thank you, Justice Cashman, as I've said, I believe we have demonstrated significant national security concerns, and I would refer you to sections two through five of our brief, and we believe the supplemental materials are also convincing and speak to the specific vulnerabilities which could be exposed," I just stared at her, waiting.

"As to your second question, while I can safely say there are strenuous investigative efforts underway, anything beyond that is, to use an old governmental saying, above my paygrade, sir."

I tilted my head just a touch, hoping she noticed, but no one else, to acknowledge the point. Her head movement in return told me my message had been delivered. She knew I wasn't trying to set her up with the second question. It was really for her boss, the attorney general, and through him, the FBI.

A question from Olive Oyl, a clarifying statement posing as a question from the chief, a hypothetical from Romona, and her half hour of pummeling was complete. She reserved no time for later, a smart move in my view. She knew it wouldn't help and might make things worse.

Next up with ten minutes each were lawyers representing NASA, the Pentagon, and the Director of National Intelligence. The last poor bastard had, I was sure, already been beaten to a pulp by other lawyers at the CIA, NSA, and DIA, all of which were probably pissed they couldn't argue themselves. His ten minutes here was going to be easy, no matter what we did to him, compared to what he'd already gone through.

A woman representing NASA went first. Romo and Perry pounded her, and then the guy representing the Pentagon, like professional tennis players hitting baseline shots with all their might, with the resounding grunts that would scare the hell out of a full-grown male moose. The guy for the Director of National Intelligence watched all this and stepped to the podium with a look that said, "take your best shot, I've already been beaten."

To my surprise, he got off easy. Maybe the brethren recognized what I had or had just worn themselves out already. At this point it hit me; Judy hadn't said a word or asked a single question. It was one of the few arguments since she'd taken the seat, where she wasn't a voluble participant.

The last hour was given over to the lawyer for the little green men gurus. If he'd been smart, and he wasn't, he would have concentrated on the winning hand he'd been dealt by the government not proving the national security claims and the high threshold for prior restraint of publication. He did a little of that, but veered off into the world of Klingon space ships and alien life on the rock they'd picked out.

Jose and the chief gently tried to get him back on track, with no success. I was able to get into my game and complete one level. Olive Oyl had, in my opinion, the best question of the day. With her grating voice and gentle manner, she destroyed any semblance of credibility he had, luckily for him, near the end of his time.

"Young man, a picture of these alien beings or the spacecraft you contend was seen would have gone a long way in convincing me that your clients have a leg to stand on regarding that part of your argument. Do you have anything like that?"

He stuttered for a good fifteen seconds, said something unintelligible to me, although maybe the stenographer made it out, and the chief put him out of his misery.

"Mr. Spock," yes, that was his real name. "Your time is up, the case is submitted," the chief said.

Now the real fun would begin.

14

We met in conference the next morning instead of waiting until Friday as we usually would. Before getting to the space case, we did a quick review of where we were on opinions.

"I'm set with the drone opinion. Judy, do you have any changes to the dissent?" I asked.

"No, I'm done also," she said.

Romo and Jose both had opinions ready to release. I had finished a concurrence on Romo's.

"We can release those on Monday, then," the chief said. "Now let's get to our case from yesterday," and he started his lecture. I zoned out and began doodling on my pad. I assume he maintained his normal lecture duration, but didn't look at my watch. The words "in summary" brought me out of my reverie. The chief thought the government had made a better case than I did, but was unwilling to stay publication. That was one.

Olive Oyl wanted to give the government the benefit of the doubt but also didn't believe they met the threshold to restrict the media outlet. My turn.

"The stay needs to be lifted immediately. The government didn't even come close to meeting their burden," I said. Romo was even more adamant than I. Firewater and Jose agreed as well. Romona leaned a little more toward the government than Olive Oyl, but also voted to let them publish.

"Whoever sent that poor girl up to argue that garbage needs an ass whupping," Perry opened with. He voted to lift the stay as well. We were down to Judy.

"I agree with Olivia. The government would ordinarily get a degree of presumption with me but they just gave us nothing. I vote to lift," she said. Nine to nothing. I smiled. Then the chief spoke.

"Thank you all. I think I will keep this opinion. With the national security implications, I think it would be best coming from the Chief Justice."

Now I wasn't smiling. The chief was the slowest writer on the court.

'Uh, Chief, a thought if I may," I couldn't just sit there. I decided to take one for the team.

"I think the critical action is to lift the stay. If not tomorrow, on Monday morning at the latest. We're also very late in the term. Clerks are leaving for future employment and various of the brethren have, uh, plans and commitments" I glanced at Judy who diverted her eyes to her pad.

"While I have no doubt that whatever you write will be outstanding and well represent our discussion today," a little butt kissing wouldn't hurt with what I was about to suggest. "I think with the urgency as well as the lateness of the term, a per curiam lifting the stay and announcing the vote, by you of course, could then be followed by your opinion and individual opinions if justices want to express their views. That would hopefully allow us to conclude the term by the end of the month. What do you think, Perry?" I wanted to get others talking before the chief could reject the idea, and thought Perry would be the most receptive.

"I agree completely. No delay, announce on Monday. This thing is a dog with fleas and we need to get 'er done and get out of here," he said.

Romo chimed in, then Firewater and Olive Oyl. The chief saw he was outmaneuvered and outvoted if we brought it to that.

"I think that's a prudent approach, Harry. I still plan to complete a full airing of my views. The case warrants that, but I'll gin up a per curiam tomorrow and we'll lift the stay and go with the announcement on Monday before announcing the decisions in the other cases."

I let out a sigh of relief and nodded in acknowledgment. Happy, but surprised I'd won, there were smiles around the table, one of the biggest on our junior justice.

Judy and I walked back to our chambers together. There was a bit of a jig in her step.

"I'm so glad you did that Harry. If the chief kept the opinion and we did this the usual way, we'd be here until August," she said.

"The speed he writes, maybe September, especially with concurrences, and it would be ridiculous to keep the stay in place that whole time," I said.

She got to her chambers, turned, winked at me, and entered. I opened my door, walked in and waved the clerks to follow me.

Walking around my desk, I dropped my portfolio filled with my chief lecture artwork from the morning, and took my suit coat off, draping it over the back of my leather chair.

"Nine to zero," I said with no preliminaries as they took their seats.

"Who's writing the opinion?" John asked.

"That's a great question. Anybody who wants to," I said, and looked out at four confused faces. I laughed.

"We're issuing a per curiam on Monday lifting the stay, announcing the result, and saying opinions will follow. The chief was dissuaded from treating this like a typical opinion due to the lateness in the term, and the need to promptly lift the stay. He indicated his intention to write an extensive opinion, which is fine. I'm going to write and lay out my views. It'll look, I guess, like a concurrence," I said.

They all nodded and looked at each other. This hadn't been handled like any other case this year, so there was no clerk with primary responsibility. We were so close to the end of the term; I knew they were wondering which of them would get stuck with the opinion.

I thought about the discussions we'd had as a group, the outstanding work left to be completed, and who had it, and reached a decision.

"Leslie, I'd like you to take this one," she looked like she'd been given the death sentence. I couldn't blame her, but she had the best understanding of the issues of the four of them.

"Don't worry, I'm going to give you detailed notes by the end of tomorrow. In fact, to prevent you from working all weekend, figure Monday morning."

"Yes sir," she said, still looking like I'd shot her dog.

"It's going to be a short opinion and we'll be finished the end of next week. Piece of cake," I said.

She nodded, but looked no more enthusiastic. The relief on the faces of the guys was obvious.

"Okay troops, back to work. The end is near."

I spent the rest of the day writing notes, sentences, sentence fragments, and precedents I wanted to cite. It wasn't hard in a case like this that wasn't a close call. There were no subtleties or nuances to parse to reach a conclusion. And since I wasn't writing it as a majority, I could let loose. I filled a half dozen pages of my note pad.

Changing my mind, I called Leslie back in. She looked a little happier than this morning, but not much.

"I know I said you weren't getting my notes until Monday, but I've got them done. You can start on it tomorrow, which gives you an extra day. You have to promise me, though, that you'll take the weekend off." I pushed the paper across the desk and continued.

"Short, simple, and most importantly, understandable to the layman is what I'm going for. This is a fundamental topic we're writing about here. It's a big deal when the government tries to muzzle the media, even ones talking about little green men and Klingon battle cruisers. I don't give a damn if the law reviews write about it or judges cite it down the road. Joe the plumber needs to be able to understand the issues. Got it?"

"Yes sir, I'll work on it tomorrow," she said, rising from her seat.

"And take the weekend off?" I double checked, raising my eyebrows at her to show I was serious.

"Yes sir, happily," she said, smiling for the first time today.

On Monday, the chief read the per curiam we'd agreed to on the space case, then the rest of the completed decisions were announced. We still had about ten outstanding, a few of which would be finished and released every couple days for the remainder of June. I read a brief summary of the drone case majority and Judy from her dissent. With the lifting of the stay on publishing whatever they were going to write about the little green men getting all the media attention, I hoped the majority and dissent by the two Cashman's, especially the sole dissent, would receive minimal attention.

Romo's opinion was next. She read a summary, and hers was followed by Jose's majority in an incredibly boring tax case. Then we adjourned with the chief noting the possibility of further opinions on Wednesday or Thursday. Normal for this time in the term, which couldn't end soon enough for me. I was laser focused on our plans for the weekend. There was light at the end of the tunnel.

15

Romo and Perry were ready for the ceremony, wearing their judicial robes. The rest of the brethren were in business attire, except for the chief who had his admiral's costume robe on, the stripes glowing under the ceiling lighting. Maybe he thought he should be suited up, like a back-up quarterback, in case of injury to Romo or Perry. No matter, I was sure the robe was less gaudy than whatever suit and tie combination was beneath it.

Our daughter was Judy's maid of honor and our son, my best man. He and I wore dark suits, my daughter a beautiful dress, and Judy's was, the only description I can manage, stunning.

The justices in attendance were snapping away with their cell phones, a very frugal wedding photographer methodology, I think. Perry had offered to hum the wedding march, but Judy declined, and the look she gave him during that conversation made it clear the subject was not negotiable.

Romo, not surprisingly, took charge of making sure the ceremony moved forward on time. She didn't put two fingers in her mouth and whistle, but close. After clearing her throat failed to quell the conversation going on in the room, she whacked the bible she had in her hand on the adjacent table to get everyone's attention. I think she wished there was a gavel handy, although it might have been used on Perry instead of to get the group's attention.

It worked, and everyone took their places. Humoring his need to be involved, we let the chief, who beamed with happiness at his inclusion, walk Judy the ten steps to the front of the room where I waited with my son. Perry did hum, but only loud enough for Romo and I to hear him. My daughter preceded Judy down the aisle, if you could call it that, and stood to her left, watching Perry with a jaundiced eye. Maybe she heard too.

Drill Sergeant Romaldini again cleared her throat and glared at the crowd. There was instant silence this time. She smiled. Then she started, using the paper she had secreted in the bible with the ceremony, or at least her version of it, written out. The only direction we gave her was keep it short.

"We are gathered here to join this man and woman in holy matrimony. This is a joyous day. Do you, Harry, take Judith to be your lawful wedded wife, to have and hold in good times and bad, sickness and health," she said, then looked at me.

"I do," I said. At this point, my life would have been in severe danger with any other answer. Now it was Perry's turn.

"Do you, Judy, take Harry, to be your wedded husband, to have and hold in good and bad times, sickness and health," he said, receiving a glare from Romo for the modifications, slight as they were, from the wording she had prepared.

"I do," Judy said.

"By the power vested in us by the Federal District of Columbia," Romo began the conclusion, which I could tell she was making up. Perry interrupted.

"And these sexy black robes," he added. Romo stomped on his foot.

Judy snickered, our daughter looked horrified, our son looked at his watch.

"I now pronounce you husband and wife. You may kiss the bride," Romo concluded. So, I did.

The reception, if you want to call it that, was also at the court. Romo insisted that she would be catering it which meant the food was better than any wedding I'd been to in my life, especially my first three. As much as I enjoyed the spread, it was more fun watching Firewater, Jose, and the Chief, who had limited experience with cuisine de Romo. From the volume of food each consumed, it appeared they enjoyed it.

The wedding gifts were a mix of prank and serious. The Chief got us a case of Silver Oak Cabernet from an excellent vintage, more appreciated by me than Judy, his taste in wine orders of magnitude better than his taste in clothing. On top of all the food, Romo's gift was a set of restaurant quality cookware and set of Global knives, which thrilled Judy and would likely result in stitches for me. Perry got Judy a t-shirt he'd had made for her. Across the front it read "First, Fourth, and Best." More seriously, he got us tickets to a dozen Nationals games. The four seats per game made his intentions obvious.

A week or so after a brief honeymoon, we split up. No, not that way. I was at my old Pennsylvania stomping grounds of Dickinson Law leading a month-long seminar program and lecturing. Judy was in England at Cambridge teaching. She had been invited shortly after her confirmation, and before she had written her first sentence as a justice, to be a guest lecturer, the Brits apparently believing any judge who could put up with multiple days of questions from the United States Senate must be smart.

Both gigs were only for a month, then we were back in the city moving into the new house Judy had found long distance while eating crumpets and drinking tea. I drove down one weekend to view it in person and walk her through it virtually via Facetime, before we made the offer. Selling the existing places was easy. Moving was a pain in the ass.

By September we were settled, and like a boxer training for their next match, we were working at reading cert petitions, getting in shape for the long conference. We were also handling our newfound notoriety. Offers were pouring in. Okay, a slight exaggeration. It's not like we were Oprah or Brad Pitt and Jennifer Anniston. Major exaggeration is more technically correct, but even three or four seemed like a flood to me.

The President invited us to a state dinner. In the past, those had been the province of the Chief Justice. It wasn't like this one was for the King of England or the Pope. No, the visiting dignitary was the President of some tiny landlocked mountain range whose name ended in "stan." There are a bunch of them, I think, and I honestly can't remember which one. Judy smoothed it over with the Chief who conveniently came up with an out-of-town judicial conference to attend, as his way of saving face for not being invited. He was gracious about it and, I'm told, felt much better after word leaked back to him of Judy telling people we were only filling in during his absence. I'm sure him learning of my falling asleep during the after-dinner toasts didn't hurt. And subsequently, the invitations resumed flowing his way.

An easy one to turn down was a joint book deal, ala Carville and Matalin. We were in our new home office and library, seated at our desks which, as I had insisted, did not look at each other. I skimmed a cert petition one of my new clerks thought had promise, or would at least make me smile. Suddenly laughter erupted from Judy's desk where she was going through a stack of mail. I hoped it wasn't the electric bill she was reacting to.

"You'll love this one. Some publisher wants us to write a joint book on married couples working together in a professional setting," she said.

"The publisher obviously doesn't know much about the court system if he or she thinks our big marble palace is a professional workplace," I said, then had a second thought. "What's the offer for the advance?"

"Forget it, Harry," she said, running it through the shredder she kept behind her desk. I was developing a major dislike for that thing and the noise it made, especially when she used it when I was concentrating on something.

A few of the television news magazine shows—few sounds better than two, which was the exact number—requested interviews in the first couple months after the wedding. We turned those down, and as we faded from the *Washington Post* gossip coverage, offers died out.

A television producer floated a "concept," as he called it that the two of us could, after retirement, host a Judge Judy type show handling divorces. As having root canal without anesthetic was more desirable to me than involvement in other people's divorces, especially after my experiences, that one was easily a hard no.

That was pretty much it for the flood unless there were some Judy didn't mention to me, which is possible; her attitude toward "monetizing" our new found "fame" being even more negative than mine.

We went into court a few days a week, starting in late August and early September. I have to admit enjoying the comfortable ride of Judy's Lexus a couple days a week, alternating driving as we did. As I hoped for, my briefcase contained a rotating selection of salami, roast beef, and similar sandwiches for lunch. Only if Judy was out of town was I forced to revert to peanut butter and jelly, although the nostalgic lunch was enjoyable now that it wasn't my everyday meal.

The new term looked like it would begin the way the last one ended, with a mix of cases, interesting and, well, stupid. The statisticians with too much time on their hands came out with their annual charts and graphs of the last term. About thirty percent of the cases we heard had a unanimous decision, which was about the average in the previous five years. Of those that weren't unanimous, it showed Judy and I were on the same side, majority or dissent, about sixty percent of the time. Since that was about the level of agreement we had choosing television shows and movies, it seemed reasonable to me.

My clerks from the term just completed term did well for themselves. The two quiet ones landed associate positions at large firms; one in DC and the other in New York City, both starting at the same salary as a Supreme Court Justice. Not bad for 30-year-olds. Leslie and John each announced their wedding engagements. The surprise—to me—was the engagements were to each other. It made me question my perceptiveness. Hell, I didn't think they even liked each other. Of course, that's probably what half the court staff thought about Judy and I before June.

They would be staying in town. John got himself a nice slot at the Justice Department in Office of Legislative Affairs, a perfect place for my budding Pennsylvania politician, and Leslie a position in the White House Counsel's office. Not too shabby. I told them their first two children should be named Harry and Judy. The best they would offer was considering those names for the cats they were thinking of getting. I'd trained them well.

The Chief Justice added another stripe to his robe and began talking about whether he should get gold braid on the shoulders. My suggestion that he go all the way, and get a powdered wig was not well received. He also developed a fondness for paisley suits. I was told by one of my new clerks, an obviously worldly and well-connected young man, that in recent poll on a Reddit page about local pimps, the chief had been voted best dressed over all the actual DC "business managers" by the working girls. Perry arranged to get a printout from the clerk and planned to present it to the Chief Justice in plaque form during our long conference.

The status of the rest of the brethren seemed stable; no Judd-like scandals in the offing as far as we knew. Romo could be a little testy when on the losing side too many times in a row and would threaten to retire and open a restaurant that would not serve ex-football players. I told her I doubted such a restaurant would withstand the inevitable court challenge that Perry would bring. She contended that since Perry would have to recuse himself from hearing the case, and all the other justices would be allowed to eat there for free, that she would win 8-0. She had a point.

I conducted an evaluation of my performance on the bench from the last term. I'd completed all levels in two games, and dabbled in a few others. After some thought, I decided to challenge myself to pay more attention…and hopefully complete three full games this coming term.

Finally, Judy and I began looking for property and building plans for our retirement home. We wanted something on a lake in the southern portion of Pennsylvania where there was less snow. It wasn't a project we were starting next month or even next year, but one we were looking at for within a decade.

I wanted to be able to fish on the lake, something I hadn't done for now going on sixteen terms on the court, and Judy needed paths for the bike she purchased. A big patio with space for grilling—well away from the house so I wouldn't set it on fire. And a least four or five bedrooms for the multiple grandchildren we were anticipating. Last hint.

Acknowledgements

My fascination with the US Supreme Court started many moons ago with the publication of *The Brethren: Inside the Supreme Court* by Bob Woodward and Scott Armstrong in 1979. The multiple shelves of books about the court I've accumulated since, and continue to add to, have not diminished my interest. More important than my incessant reading on the court was my incredible Editor, Sarah Piccini, and some special readers: wife Michelle, and daughter Megan, and an old friend and amazing writer, Hildy Morgan. While this is clearly a work of fiction, I tried not to take too many liberties with court functions, but invariably there were some. Hopefully these will be forgiven by any "insiders" who might scrutinize this work. Any errors or omissions are solely mine.

Made in United States
North Haven, CT
08 September 2023